SO
TALK
TO
ME

Marina Johnson

Copyright © Marina Johnson 2019

Tamarillas Press

All Rights Reserved. No part of this publication may be reproduced or transmitted in any form or by any means, electronic or mechanical, including photocopy, recording, or any information storage and retrieval system, without permission from the author.

This book is a work of fiction. All characters, locations, businesses, organisations and situations in this publication are either a product of the author's imagination or used fictitiously. Any resemblance to real persons, living or dead, is purely coincidental.

Cover image: © Canva
Design: © Marina Johnson 2019

ISBN: 9781793476234

For PG and CJ, you know why.

Other books by Marina Johnson

Fat Girl Slim

A Confusion of Murders

Prologue

Mind the gap.

The station platform is full; commuters huddled inside bulky quilted coats and muffled in scarves, clutching briefcases and handbags tightly to their bodies to keep out the cold, damp, air.

Their tired, pinched faces are turned towards the tracks for the tell-tale sign of an approaching train; willing it to arrive so they can begin their morning commute.

The digital sign blinks and a gush of wind blows through the station as a train approaches.

The crowd surge forward as one and the mechanical clank of the train is heard as it slows down on entering the station, the crowd mentally readies itself for the jostling for a seat before the train has even stopped.

Mind the gap.

A moment of confusion; a muffled cry is heard as the train screeches to a shuddering halt and the doors open with a whoosh. The swell of people flows onto the train through the open doors but further up the platform the crowd are hanging back and an unnatural stillness has settled over them. At the front of the train the driver's cab door is flung open and he clambers onto the platform and stands immobile on shaky legs, both hands held over his face.

The sound of a woman's shrill scream rings out and a man's voice commands hoarsely, 'Someone call an ambulance!'

The crowd shuffle, uncertain what to do. They nudge back as the heavy thump of feet is heard when three uniformed figures thunder down the platform.

And then a shriek of horror from a woman as she approaches the stricken train driver to offer assistance. She stands clutching her hand to her mouth as she looks down onto the tracks in front of the train.

'Someone's jumped! Oh my God, someone's jumped!'

Chapter 1

Josie

Our house is a sad house.

I'm sad, Dad's sad. Even the dog's sad.

We don't walk around crying with sad faces, moaning and wailing – quite the opposite really. We paste happyish expressions on and smile bravely and say things like *I'm fine* and *I'm alright,* but we're *so* not.

We used to be really happy, until Mum left us and then we were very unhappy for quite a long time but now we're at the *we have to get over it and carry on* stage that the whole world expects us to be at. You know, *the getting on with life* stage. We're not at that stage at all but we're good at pretending. Except Skipper (the dog), he's not so good at pretending. He was Mum's dog and I don't think his tail has wagged properly since she's been gone. We get a half-hearted wag when we come home and then he seems to remember that we're not mum and he trots off dejectedly and flops down into his basket with a big sigh. Maybe if we keep pretending, we'll start to believe we're alright if we keep doing it; sort of *fake it 'til you make it*. I can't imagine I ever will be alright but I have to carry on pretending, for Dad's sake.

So here we are standing in the hall at the bottom of the stairs and I'm ready to go but I'm waiting for Dad to finish preening himself in the mirror. He's fiddling around adjusting his tie in the round fish eye wall mirror that distorts his face and makes his nose look enormous.

'You're not wearing *that* are you?' I say.

'Well, yes, I thought I would. What's wrong with it?' Dad looks all round eyed and surprised at me.

More like what's right with it. *Beyond* embarrassing.

'You don't need to wear a suit and a tie,' I say with a sigh. 'You're not meeting the Queen. It's just a college open evening. In fact, I don't even know why you have to come, I'm seventeen, not a kid. It's not as if I'm at *school*.'

'I like to look smart.' He tightens the knot and then thinks better of it and loosens it again. 'And you know why I'm coming so let's not start all that again.'

I grab my Parka from the peg and pull it on, zip it up to my chin and pull the hood up over my head.

'Hurry *up*. I just want to get this stupid meeting over with.'

Dad stops fussing in the mirror and turns around and looks down at me for a moment and then wraps his arms round me and holds me tightly in a bear hug. My nose is being squashed into his chest and I wriggle my face free so I can breathe.

'You're a funny little thing. I just want to be there for you, because I let you down last time. I promise I won't embarrass you in front of your friends.' He says it in a sad sort of voice so I allow myself to be hugged. We stand like this for a bit and after a few minutes I duck out from his arms and go to the front door and yank it open.

'I've told you, I haven't got any friends. Everyone thinks I'm a weirdo. Now come *on*.'

Frogham Community College is an ugly grey oblong building of four floors with what seems like hundreds of windows that have wooden panels underneath them. The panels are all different colours and in different stages of peeling. Despite the jolly colours it's a drab looking affair and, in an attempt to pretty it up a bit there's a wrought iron sculpture of a dolphin in front of the entrance doors. What a dolphin has to do with anything I have no idea. It's surrounded by pebbles stuck in cement to deter anyone from getting too close, although someone has managed to spray paint their tag on it.

Of course the car park was full when we finally arrived so we had to park miles away in a side street and walk here. We got battered around by the wind and rain in the ten minutes it took us to get here and Dad and I squeeze through the double doors into the college with a feeling of relief. We can hardly get through the doors for the throng of wet, noisy people in the hall and it seems like everyone is shouting. I look at Dad and he's trying unsuccessfully to flatten his hair down with his hands; the wind has whipped it into a mass of unruly curls and the more he flattens it the springier it gets.

'Should have bought an umbrella. I look like Ronald McDonald.'

'You should get a parka like me. You can put the hood up then.' I only say this to wind him up, he wouldn't be seen dead in any coat that has a hood.

We push and shove our way through the mass of people and I pull my hood further down over my eyes but I can still sense that people are looking at me. I look down at the floor and follow Dad's feet as he battles his way through.

The hall is huge with a stage at the opposite end to the doors and it smells of rubber, cooked cabbage and damp people. I don't know why it should smell of cooked cabbage as the college canteen is at the other end of the building.

'Where do we go, Josie?' Dad stops suddenly and turns around and megaphones at me.

'Up the end,' I hiss at him, nearly falling over because he's stopped so suddenly.

'Where?' he shouts as he leans down and ducks to look underneath my hood at me.

For God's sake. The embarrassment.

'Up there.' I point to the end of the hall. 'Stop talking to me. I *told* you not to talk to me.'

Dad throws back his head and laughs loudly while I try to make myself invisible inside my coat. When he finally stops laughing, he turns on his heel and continues fighting his way through and I follow him as he bounces down the hall. I try to make myself as small as possible but I know it's not working. *Everyone* is looking at us. Why did he have to come? He can't do anything quietly. Hardly anyone else's parents are here, most have come on their own. I should have stayed at home, pretended I was ill.

'Is that her? Is that Miss Bradley?' he shouts over his shoulder.

'Stop shouting.' So irritating.

'What?' he shouts even louder over the babble of the hall.

'I said. STOP SHOUTING.'

The second the words have left my mouth the hall falls silent and everyone turns and looks at me. We come to a halt as Dad stops to scan the hall for Miss Bradley.

I don't move and keep looking straight ahead at Dad's back but out of the corner of my eye I can see one of the Clackers. I slowly move my head to be confronted by Shana looking straight at me with a smirk on her face. She's clacking chewing gum around her mouth and pouting for all she's worth.

'Hey, Josie,' she calls out and makes a beeline for me, walking towards me with that stupid flat-footed ballet walk that she thinks makes her look cute.

'Is this your Dad?' she says as she plants herself in front of him. She flutters her eyelashes up at Dad and pouts even more. The smell of the sweet candy bubble gum that she always chews wafts over as she speaks.

'Oh, Hello,' says Dad, putting his hand out to shake Shana's hand. Yes, he actually puts his hand out. 'Nice to meet you, er…aren't you going to introduce me to your friend, Josie?'

I turn my back to Shana and grab Dad's arm and yank him quickly away. 'We're late so you'll have to excuse us,' I say to Shana as I drag Dad past her.

'OMG.' She shrieks, 'You're like, *so* funny Josie, you sound like you're, what, twenty-five or something.' She puts her hands on her hips and clacks the gum around her mouth.

I ignore her completely and put my hand on Dad's back and push him past her. 'Just keep going. And stop showing me up,' I hiss at him. I didn't expect him to move so quickly and nearly fall over where I've shoved him so hard. I sneak a peek out of the corner of my eye; Shana is watching us and grinning.

I spy Miss Bradley sitting at a table near the stage and pray that no one gets there before us. If I keep shoving Dad forward, we can get it over with and go home.

'Ah, Mr Sparkes, how lovely to meet you.' Miss Bradley sees us arrive and jumps up off her chair and holds her hand out. 'I've heard so much about you.'

Liar. I've hardly spoken to her and certainly never about Dad.

'Have you?' says Dad, looking pleased and shaking her hand. He pulls the chair out from the desk and settles himself down opposite her.

'Aren't you going to sit down Josie?' Miss Bradley looks at me.

'Do I have to?'

She looks a bit uncertain. 'Well, you don't have to...'

Dad pats the chair next to him. 'Come on, Josie, sit down.'

'No. You wanted to talk to her, so talk to her but I'm not getting involved. I told you this before we left. I'll be over there when you've finished.'

I march over to the front of the stage and pretend to be engrossed in a crappy art display. I feel a bit mean. It came out all wrong, I didn't mean to sound so rude and childish.

'Didn't know you were coming.' A voice next to me makes me jump.

Biro, probably my only friend at college, or anywhere actually, has appeared next to me. He looks down at me with eyes that seem massive through the jam jar bottom lenses of his glasses.

'My Dad's over there talking to Miss Bradley.' I turn and nod my head in their direction.

'What, the bloke with the checked suit on?'
'Don't.'
'What?'

'Don't mention the suit. Or the tie. Or the hair.'

'S'not that bad. Sort of retro. Isn't brown the new black?'

I look up at him, his big owl-like eyes are twinkling and he's trying not to laugh. It's okay though; he's laughing with me, not *at* me.

'He has the worst dress sense in the world. Ever. Apart from you,' I say with a smile.

'Nothing wrong with my dress sense.'

I look at him; black bobble hat – okay, black scarf wrapped around his face – okay, fake fur coat and red doc martins – not okay.

'Where did you get that coat anyway?'

He strokes the fur fondly. 'Charity shop. Bargain. Five quid. Smells a bit though.'

'Sleeves are a bit short too.'

He stretches his arms out to show his jumper cuffs a good six inches longer than the coat sleeves.

'Starting a new trend. Think it must have belonged to a woman.'

Biro and I met on our first day; two fellow weirdos. I was sitting alone at lunch, trying to look as if I wasn't bothered about being on my own and chewing the same mouthful of sandwich that just wouldn't go down. Biro dumped his lunch tray onto the table and sat down next to me and proceeded to shovel spaghetti Bolognese into his mouth. He wolfed the whole plate down in minutes then wiped the back of his hand across his mouth and picked up a bottle of Coke.

'A levels or BTEC?' he'd said between slurps.

'GCSE re-sits,' I'd said.

'Which ones?'

'All of them.'

That's how we met. Biro really doesn't care that he's

not one of the in crowd; he's completely comfortable with how he is and doesn't even notice if he's getting laughed at, he enjoys being different.

Not like me.

I look over at Dad and Miss Bradley, deep in conversation; I wonder how much longer they'll be.

'Your parents here?' I ask Biro.

'Na. Made sure of it. Never told them about it.'

Idiot, why didn't I think of that?

'Isn't that your mate over there?' I follow his eyes to see Ellie standing with Stacey and Shana.

'No mate of mine. She's a Clacker now. One of the gang.'

'Yeah, I see she's copied the eyebrows. And the pout.'

Ellie and I used to be best friends. Right from our first day at school. We still speak; we've haven't argued or anything but we're not close anymore. I'm not sure what happened. Ellie changed but I didn't and maybe that's the problem. I never got into the whole make up and boyfriend thing, even Mum used to say I had an *old head on young shoulders*. I can't help it, it's just the way I am. I had a brief period when I tried to fit in; slapped the make-up on and tried to talk like everyone else but people can smell a fake a mile off. And that's what I was, a fake. So I just have to be me: a weirdo. Stacey started calling me the professor because of the way I speak until I pointed out that I'd failed every single one of my GCSEs.

Ellie puts up her hand and gives me a wave; I must have been staring without realising, I tend to do that. Which all adds to the weirdo label. I don't blame her for defecting, she wants to fit in and be like everyone else. Who wants to be the odd one out like me? I give a half-hearted wave back and turn to Biro.

'What have you come for if your parents aren't here?'

'Going to have a chat to my music tutor, then I'm going home. Only came so it'd look like I cared, 'cos I want to use the music room. I've got some people auditioning for my band tomorrow and I can't use the pub 'cos there's a do on. And anyway, I don't want my dad poking his nose in. You got anything planned for after?'

'No, nothing. Just going home.'

'The 'rents have got an open mic evening. Do you want to come? Might be a laugh.'

Biro's parents run a pub; it's a converted house in the middle of a row of terraced houses with a bar not much bigger than my bedroom.

'Could do,' I say casually but inside I feel ridiculously pleased that he's asked me, if it wasn't for Biro, I'd never leave the house apart from going to college.

'Ask your Dad, too.'

I look up at him.

'What?'

Biro and I are squashed between the bar and the door to the toilets. The place is rammed with people and a bearded, middle aged, long haired hippie is thumping a guitar and doing a very bad version of George Michael's "Faith".

'I'd give it up if I was him,' shouts Biro.

I nod and take a slurp of my J20. Biro takes a long swallow of his bottle of coke which I know he laced with a good few measures of vodka when his Dad wasn't looking. I don't have any in mine; don't have any tolerance for alcohol at all. We didn't ask Dad; Biro was

11

only joking but that's the thing with me, I'm not very good at knowing if people are joking or not.

Biro's Dad leans across the bar, 'Alright chick?'

'I'm fine, thank you, Mr Birowski.'

'Charlie, chick, call me Charlie. Want another drink?'

'No, I'm good, thank you.'

'I'll have one, Pa.' Biro bangs his empty bottle down on the bar.

'No, you won't son, you've had enough of my vodka.' He whisks the bottle away and drops it with a clang into a bin under the bar. 'And stop calling me Pa.'

'I haven't had any vodka.'

'Yes, you have. I wasn't born yesterday. If I lose my license it'll be your fault and I'll have your guts for garters. Anyway, make yourself useful and go and check the gents – make sure they're decent.'

Biro pulls a face. 'Do I have to?'

'Yes, you do. I'm too busy and there's no way I'm letting your mother go in there. Just flush the toilets and open the window if it needs it.'

Biro pulls a face and reluctantly leaves the bar and saunters across to the back door. The toilets are out the back through a dark, damp corridor, I think they may have been outside at one time. I never use them if I can help it; they're full of spiders and are freezing cold.

Within minutes Biro comes back and resumes his position leaning on the bar next to me.

'Okay?' I ask.

'Rank. Don't know what's difficult about flushing a toilet but no one in here seems to have that skill.' He bangs on the bar to get Charlie's attention.

'Pa! Do I get a drink now?'

'Yeah. But you're only having coke. Gents okay?'

'Fantastic, there's nothing I like more than the sight

of another bloke's shit bobbing around with dog ends floating on the top.' He takes the offered bottle of coke. 'Highlight of my evening.'

Charlie laughs and winks at me and turns to serve another customer.

'Disgusting,' mutters Biro taking a slurp of his coke.

I laugh at the look on his face and after a moment he can't help himself and joins in.

'You're lucky you're not a bloke, we're a gross lot.'

The faint sound of applause interrupts us as the George Michael wannabe finally takes the hint and gives the microphone back to the MC and sits down.

The MC clears his throat. 'Now, Ladies and Gentleman, a treat for us all. Our very own landlord, Charlie, is going to give us his rendition of Stairway to Heaven, put your hands together...'

Charlie comes out from behind the bar and weaves his way to the microphone accompanied by whistles and table thumps. The MC hands him the microphone and Charlie takes it with a beaming smile.

Biro drains his bottle of coke in one swallow and bangs it down on the bar.

'C'mon. Time to go. X Box is calling. See if you can beat me.'

'Oh. Okay. If you like.'

'I do like.' He looks across at Charlie who points the microphone at Biro and winks at him.

Biro rolls his eyes at me. 'And you thought *your* Dad was embarrassing.'

'Don't you want to know what she said?'

We've just got home. Dad picked me up from Biro's and I wondered how long it would be before we'd have to have "the conversation". We chatted about the pub and the open mic night in the car but not the college meeting but I knew it was only a matter of time.

'Not really.'

'Josie, don't you think we should talk about it?'

I hang my coat up and keep my back to him so I don't have to look him in the eye.

'Nothing to talk about,' I say, hoping that he'll give up.

I can sense he hasn't moved and I turn around and he's standing in front of me with his arms folded.

'Look. You need to face up to things, you can't avoid your feelings forever. Miss Bradley thinks seeing a counsellor would really help you.'

'I'm not avoiding anything. I'm not going to see a shrink and that's the end of it.' I fold my arms across my body to emphasise the point.

Dad sighs. 'She's not a shrink, she's a counsellor and she might be able to help. Miss Bradley says she refers students to the college counselling service all the time. There's no shame in it.'

'I don't care. I don't need any help.'

'You do. You know you do. You need to talk things through, about Mum and what happened in your exams.'

'I don't need to talk about it, I'm fine. And people are allowed to fail exams you know.'

'You're not fine and you didn't fail them.'

I unfold my arms and squeeze past Dad and start up the stairs. 'I'm off to bed, got to get up in the morning.'

'Just think about it,' he calls after me.

'Night,' I call over my shoulder.

'Night, sweetheart.' He sounds dejected and I feel bad. Again.

I close my bedroom door and lean my back against it

and let out a sigh of relief. The last thing I need to do is to talk to a counsellor; I can't talk about Mum, if I start talking I might not be able to stop and then it'll all come out. I can't tell anyone the truth.

Especially not Dad.

Chapter 2

Robbie

It's hard being a single parent, really hard, and it's not something that I ever thought I'd have to do. I'm struggling and there isn't a minute goes by when I don't miss Nessa and wish she was here.

But all the wishing in the world isn't going to bring her back, is it?

I'll be the first to admit that I wasn't much use to Josie in the first few months we were on our own, and I let her down, big time, I know I did. But things are a bit better now, I'm slowly getting on top of things and getting us a new kind of normal.

And our Josie's always been very serious; even as a five-year-old. She's never been your run of the mill kid, an old head on young shoulders, Nessa used to say. Deep, that's how a lot of people describe her, she gives things a lot of thought, thinks things through. She certainly doesn't take after me that's for sure. But even though she's always been a thoughtful kid she used to laugh and giggle and she was funny; dry, but so funny. The three of us used to have such fun, Nessa and Josie used to laugh at *me*, at me pulling faces and my dress sense, and I used to play to it and I could always get a laugh out of Josie even when she turned into a moody teenager.

But Josie rarely laughs now. She might paste a smile on her face when I talk to her or if she catches me looking at her but she doesn't fool me. Seventeen-year-olds should be out having fun and enjoying themselves, going to parties and hanging out with their mates; having a laugh. She should be enjoying being young and having a good time, but she's not.

She doesn't even swear, says things like "for God's sake," I mean, I don't want her cussing and swearing but Jesus, she's seventeen going on fifty. My brother, well, half-brother, Ralph - same mum, different dad - he loves Josie to bits, would do absolutely anything for her and treats her like the daughter he never had. He won't have a word said against her - even he says, 'Robbie mate, you need to get her to see someone, get some therapy or something – she's seventeen and she behaves like our bleedin' maiden aunt, it ain't right.' Which just shows he's as worried as me because he doesn't believe in counselling or 'talking bollocks,' as he calls it. I keep wishing Nessa was here because she'd know what to do and then I realise what a stupid thing that is to think because if she was here Josie wouldn't be like this, would she?

It's a two-way thing, Josie and her uncle Ralph, she adores him even though he's the most un-pc person you could ever meet and can be downright obnoxious at times. She used to love listening to his newspaper stories (he's the editor of the Frogham Herald) and all about the people he's come across. She'd write these little articles for him, you know, made up stuff but Ralph says she's got a flair for it and she even talked about becoming a reporter. But that was before Nessa died. Now she just shrugs when I ask her what she wants to do, like it doesn't matter. Ralph's tried talking to her but she stonewalls him like she does me.

For a while I thought maybe we should move house, start afresh. But we have so many happy memories in this house why move to get rid of one bad one? And I don't think it would work anyway, you can't run away from things and we always loved it here. It was a dream come true when Nessa and I bought it – we'd thought we'd made it. Josie was a toddler when we moved here and it's the only home she's ever known.

Ralph moved to Frogham first; he kept telling us what a lovely place it was, family friendly, plenty of jobs. Nessa and I were a bit disbelieving, thought it was the back of beyond and couldn't imagine wanting to live anywhere but London and couldn't believe Ralph would think otherwise. So we visited, because Ralph kept on and on, then we could see what he meant. It was so much quieter than London, a fraction of the traffic; five minutes and you're in the countryside. And people actually *talk* to you when you're out for a walk with the dog. So we sold up and we couldn't believe it when the proceeds from our tiny one bed flat in London bought us this house, it felt like a mansion to us. I tell you, we couldn't believe our luck.

No, moving's not the answer. Besides, we'd struggle to find anywhere better, it's a great house in a lovely area with good neighbours.

Apart from the serial killer who used to live across the road.

But he's in prison now, the Frogham Throttler, and he won't be coming out any time soon. I've passed his house and seen builders putting up a massive extension on the front, nearly doubling the size of it so I'm guessing someone's bought it. I wonder if they know who lived there? Anyway, lightening doesn't strike twice, hardly likely to be two serial killers in a place the size of Frogham is there? Although I think Ralph would quite like it if there was. A good murder sells a ton of newspapers, he says. Callous sod.

But Josie? I'm at a loss to be honest.

Like Ralph says, maybe if she sees a counsellor it'll help. She can get it all off her chest. Because she won't talk to me, I've tried but she won't. Insists that she's fine. I keep telling her; it's alright not to be okay, it's not a sign of weakness but I can tell she's not listening. She hasn't even cried, not that I've seen anyway. I've cried plenty, get it out, that's my motto. I don't know that it does help because I feel pretty shit when I'm doing it but I honestly don't think I could hold it in. It bothers me that Josie's bottling it all up and my way of thinking is that it's got to come out, sooner or later, and the longer she holds it in the worse it'll be.

I wish that I could help her and it breaks my heart that I can't, but if she won't let me in, I can't. I just can't bear to see her so sad, and when she puts that brave face on it makes it even worse. I always used to get a laugh out of her with my daftness. And if that failed then I knew she would definitely laugh at my dress sense, yet the night of the Open Evening she was embarrassed by me, by what I was wearing. It never used to bother her what other people said, she used to say everyone was entitled to their opinion. She thought my outfits were hilarious even when Nessa didn't. She'd say, 'Dad, wear that shirt with the frogs on,' or 'I haven't seen that yellow striped jumper for a while, about time you wore it again.' She's always had her own mind, which she still has, but now she seems ashamed and embarrassed by it.

She wouldn't even sit with me and talk to her tutor. Point blank refused. Her tutor says she's doing okay, academically - not that I needed telling, it's a fact that Josie is super clever and she could do her re-sits right now and pass them all with flying colours. She has a photographic memory; not instant, she has to think through things but once she's seen something, she remembers it forever. She should have passed her exams easily last time – and I'm to blame for what happened, I was too busy feeling sorry for myself when I should have been thinking about her. She doesn't need to go to college to swot up so she can pass the exams, I persuaded her to go because I thought she'd make new friends, make a new start.

She keeps telling me that she hasn't got any friends because they all think she's a weirdo. If only she knew how it cuts through me like a knife when she says that. She used to have loads of friends and they thought a lot of her, I could tell, especially Ellie. Now the only one she ever mentions is Stefan. Biro, he calls himself; seems a pleasant enough lad although he does wear some odd stuff and that's saying something coming from someone with my dress sense. He had a fur coat on the other night that looked like he got it off his mum. I mean, there are limits.

That's the other thing – Josie lives and dies in that bloody Parka coat. Made me buy it for her for Christmas and I don't think it's been off her back since. Jeans, baggy jumper and that Parka; you could easily mistake her for a boy until you see her pretty little face.

'Put something else on,' I tell her, nice clothes give you a boost, make you feel better. I know what I'm talking about, when Josie and I were first on our own I had a job to get myself out of bed and into work in the mornings, never mind caring what I wore. But after a while you realise that life goes on, you have to get out there and just *live,* keep going through the motions even though you don't feel like it and then after a while it's not so hard.

When Nessa died, I wanted to curl up and die myself. If I could have lain down and willed myself to go to sleep and never wake up, I would have. The rumours that went around didn't help either; I know people like a good gossip but they don't realise how hurtful it is to the people involved. I tried to keep the details from Josie but the inquest was reported in the papers although obviously not in the Herald, Ralph wouldn't print *anything.* It was all over the internet though. Just our luck one of the nationals decided to do a spread on "jumper" deaths just after Nessa died. It was unbearable. Some nosey parker reporter even turned up at our house asking if we wanted to do an interview, he even shouted through the letterbox. He wouldn't go away, just stood outside ringing the bell. I had to ring Ralph eventually; couldn't trust myself to open the door and speak to the guy 'cos I think I'd have killed him. I don't know what Ralph said to him but he soon went away.

I can't blame the Coroner because they have to look into all of the possibilities and suicide was one of them, even thought there was no suicide note. Apparently not that many people leave them. So, although the verdict was accidental death there are always nasty types that say it was suicide; that she didn't just stumble, that it wasn't just the most awful, most rotten bad luck.

I had to talk to Josie about the inquest because the outcome was all over the internet so it was pointless trying to hide it. I didn't let her attend, even though she wanted to, because I thought she was too young. Now I think maybe I should have let her go because she found out anyway. There was so much gossip about it being suicide and I hope that I put Josie's mind at rest; I told her that there was no way Nessa would had left us deliberately because she was happy, we were all happy.

I spent the first few months after Nessa died torturing and blaming myself when I should have been helping Josie. You know, the what ifs – what if I'd said to Nessa, don't go to London for that meeting, or what if I'd driven her instead of her taking the train, or why didn't she stand at the back and not near the front. Kept running it over and over; wishing somehow, I could turn back the clock and change things.

If only.

Eventually I pulled myself together because it's not just about me is it? I have to be around for Josie, make things right for her, see her happy again. But I know I wasn't there for her as much as I should have been to start with.

We're always going to miss Nessa. That's a fact. And we will never, ever get over losing her, that's also a fact. In a perfect world Josie would have been old herself before she lost her mum which would have still been horrible but that's things in the right order, if you know what I mean. But it is what it is and life goes on and Josie has her whole life in front of her and I've got a lot of mine in front of me, too. I may seem ancient and decrepit to Josie but I'm only 43 and I intend to make the most of it and I want her to make the most of her life as well. I can't replace Nessa, can't see myself ever being with anyone else but if there's one thing I do know it's that you never know what's around the corner, life is full of surprises and not all of them good.

Anyway, enough navel gazing, time to take the dog for a walk.

'Come on, Skipper. Walkies.' I rattle his lead at him and he looks up at me with disinterest from his basket, his stumpy little tail giving the very faintest of wags.

'Walkies.' Bit louder this time and he looks up at me with those sad eyes and sighs.

I think he may need a counsellor too.

Chapter 3

Josie

Mr Borden is sitting in the chair opposite me and smiling. He's too close; one of his crossed knees is only millimetres from mine. Will it look too obvious if I move my chair back? He's too close. His legs are so long they seem to take up half the room.

How did I let myself be persuaded to see a student counsellor, I ask myself for the millionth time?

Dad kept on about it so much that in the end I gave in just to shut him up, I knew that he wasn't going to let it go until I gave in. I decided that I'd just not bother turning up for the appointment and then I'd just be forgotten about and put down as a no show.

No such luck.

Mr Borden came and got me out of my maths tutorial.

Yes. He actually came and interrupted the tutorial, knocked on the door, stuck his head round it and asked the tutor if I could be excused as I'd forgotten about my appointment.

The humiliation. Absolutely *everyone* looked at me. I got up from my desk and meekly walked out of the classroom, too mortified to even argue. I could feel everyone's eyes on me as I walked to the door and I knew the whispering would start the minute I'd gone. Really, there should be a law against it, I thought counselling was supposed to be confidential. Okay, Mr Borden didn't say it was for counselling but he did say appointment so everyone pretty much guessed. Mrs Bundy, the maths tutor, looked surprised and slightly uncomfortable or was that my imagination? Now the whole college knows that I'm having counselling, as if everyone didn't think I was weird enough.

I could *kill* Dad.

And that wasn't the only shock.

Dad told me that the counsellor was going to be a woman.

Mr Borden is definitely not a woman, he's a man. A very hot man, to be honest. Yes, he is really old, at least twenty-five or thirty, but he's also very handsome and I just can't see myself being able to talk to someone so good looking; I can't even look at him without blushing.

I'd trailed along the corridor behind him for what seemed like forever while he chatted and every so often he turned and checked I was still there in case I'd run away. And I did think about it; running away, but I had a horrible feeling he would come and find me so I didn't. Every time he turned, I'd blush even more and then he'd do that really nice smile, showing his perfect teeth, like he totally understood how I was feeling and then I'd blush even more until I thought my face was going to burst into flames.

'I'm so glad you've agreed to come along, Josie. I've been a student counsellor for some time and I'm sure that I'll be able to help with whatever's troubling you.'

I may have agreed in theory but I had no intention

of actually turning up. I'm sure he won't be able to help at all. I can't even look at him without my face turning beetroot; how could someone so gorgeous possibly understand what a normal person feels like? And a poor version of normal too. He should be a model not a counsellor, why would he want to be a counsellor when he could be anything he wanted? It doesn't make any sense to me.

Obviously, I don't say any of this because I've decided I won't speak at all. He can't make me speak; he can come and drag me out of a lesson and embarrass me but he can't actually make me say anything. I'll sit here for half an hour and not say a word. I don't have to tell him anything.

'Are you sure you're comfortable? Not too cold?' He puts his hand on the rusting radiator behind him to check it's working.

I shake my head and push my hands deeper in the pockets of my Parka.

'Okay. Now, most people think that talking to a stranger is hard.' He uncrosses his legs and leans forward, elbows resting on his knees. 'But I promise you, once you start, it'll get a lot easier.'

Too close. He's much too close. I need my personal space. How long are his legs for God's sake? I wish I'd moved my chair backwards before I sat down; it's too late now.

'I don't know you, you don't know me. What happens in Vegas stays in Vegas.'

He sees the blank look on my face. 'What I mean is, whatever's said in this room is totally confidential.'

Silence.

'And, sometimes a stranger's perspective can be surprisingly helpful.'

I wonder if I can sneak a look at my watch. How long have I been here? Ten minutes? Maybe twenty more to get through. I stare at the floor and wonder if I can count the seconds off in my head. I scrutinise the carpet; murky green and corded with scattered bald patches interspersed with tiny white splashes. Is that paint? This office doesn't look like it's been painted for a very long time.

'So, Josie, talk to me. Tell me, why do you think you're here?'

He makes me jump when he speaks, I'd almost forgotten where I was. He's staring at me intently, waiting for an answer. To not answer suddenly seems extremely rude and he seems so nice and he's only doing his job after all. I decide that I don't have to tell him anything *real*, just tell him what he wants to hear.

'I'm here because my Dad insisted, Mr Borden.'

He smiles. 'Call me Adam, please. I take it from your answer that you don't want to be here?'

'No, not really.'

'That's not unusual. A lot of people feel the way you do. A lot of people think counselling's a waste of time and that talking about things can't do any good. It's also quite difficult to start talking about things that are causing you pain, but once you start, you'll find that it gets easier.'

Silence.

'Okay.' Another smile. 'I'll start, shall I? I understand that your mother passed away last year?'

'Yes.' Don't ask me how I feel about it. Just don't. The room suddenly seems very warm. I want to take my coat off, but I can't move and feel rooted to the chair. And I know that even if I take it off, I'll only want to put it back on again.

'Last February wasn't it?' he prompts.

I nod.

'Nearly a year ago?'

I nod again. Just. Shut. Up.

'I understand her death was very sudden?'

'Yes.'

'Must have been a terrible shock.'

Does he really want me to agree with him?

'Would you say that you were close to your mother?'

I answer, in spite of myself. 'Very.'

He pauses and scribbles a few notes in his notepad but has it tipped away from me so I can't see what he's written. I feel suddenly annoyed that he's writing things down about me.

'I thought you said whatever's said here stays in this room? Why are you writing things down?' I blurt out.

'Just the odd word, Josie, to remind myself of our conversation. It wouldn't mean anything to anyone else.' He closes the notepad and places it on the desk and puts the pen on top with an air of finality.

'So. Do you want to talk about what happened with your GCSE exams?'

'No.'

'Would I be right in saying that you were expected to achieve A stars in every one of your subjects?'

He's staring at me and I feel my face start to redden again.

'You can tell me Josie, really, I've heard it all.'

'I failed them.'

'That's not quite true is it?'

'It is. I failed every one of them.'

'Why do you think that was?'

I shrug.

'Was it because you were angry? With your mother?

For what she'd done?'

'She hadn't done anything!' I almost shout at him.

'She died, Josie – were you angry at her for dying?'

I exhale the breath that I didn't realise I was holding. For a horrible moment I thought he *knew*.

'Anyone sitting here?'

'Not unless they're the invisible man,' Biro says drily.

Shana sniffs and puts her lunch tray on the table next to Biro and Stacey and Ellie shuffle around to the other side of the table and do the same.

I knew I wouldn't get away with it. I curse myself for being so stupid as to sit at a table with spare seats. I push my plate away from me; I can't eat anything now because I know the questions are going to start and I'll just keep chewing and chewing and it won't go down.

I look across the table at Biro; he's oblivious and wolfing down an enormous baguette. He doesn't understand about the Clackers when I tell him they make snide comments and make me feel uncomfortable. 'Just tell them to fuck off and mind their own,' he says incredulously, 'It's not like they're your friends or anything.'

He's completely right, they're not my friends but I can't do what he says; I haven't got the guts to come out and say something like that and although I hate them, I don't want them as outright enemies.

'So,' says Shana, nibbling delicately on a lettuce leaf, taking care not to spoil her perfectly applied lipstick, 'Who was the guy who came and got you out of maths?'

They know who it was, they just want to make me suffer by making me tell them.

'I know who it was,' Stacey interrupts before I have a chance to answer.

Shana looks at her and says sarcastically, 'Wow, Josie, you said that without even opening your mouth.'

Stacey looks momentarily confused. 'I do, too,' she whines in her fake American voice, 'It's the college shrink.'

'OMG Stacey you are such a dullard sometimes.'

Shana rolls her eyes at Stacey and turns back to me. I ignore her and pull my phone out of my pocket and pretend to be engrossed in it.

'So Josie,' Shana says with fake concern in her voice, 'I didn't realise you were seeing a shrink, anything we can help with, hun? You know we're always here to help. You only have to ask.'

Yeah, so you can get all of the gory details, embellish them and broadcast it around the entire college.

'Thanks,' I say, 'but it's only about why I failed my exams. He's giving me coping mechanisms so I don't get so nervous next time and mess it up again.' I sound so convincing I almost believe it myself.

Shana looks deflated, she was expecting more. She frowns slightly in disappointment, her thick, black pencilled-in eyebrows joining closer together like giant caterpillars. Stacey just looks vacant like she normally does. Ellie, though, I can see that she's not fooled at all. She can't meet my eyes and is looking down at the table.

'Yeah, I thought it was something like that. Some of the other guys…' Shana waves her hand around the hall. 'Were saying they thought it was because you had a few, um, you know, mental health issues.' She looks at me and I realise she expects some sort of answer.

'No, I'm fine, thanks,' I say with a tight little smile.

'Yeah, that's what I said. I said, guys, she's fine, that's *her* normal.'

'Shana...' Biro starts to speak but I stop him by standing up and simultaneously kicking his leg hard under the table.

'Anyway, must go,' I say. 'Catch you all later.'

Shana smiles nastily and Stacey looks at me quizzically. Ellie looks at me unsmilingly and puts her hand up in a sort of wave.

On the way past I grab a handful of Biro's coat as he's getting up and haul him out of the chair after me. He walks along by my side silently and waits until we're out of earshot and then he turns to me angrily.

'Why do you let them treat you like that?'

'I've told you, it's easier.'

'Tell 'em to fuck off, you're hardly going to miss them. Bunch of cows.'

'No. It's fine. I can cope with them like that. If I really fall out with them, they'll really have it in for me.'

Biro is silent and I realise he's fuming.

'I'm sorry, Biro. It's just my way of dealing with them. I know I'm annoying.'

He looks at me with a funny expression on his face and hooks his arm around my neck and pulls me towards him.

'You don't need to be sorry. I'm not annoyed with you, it's them. Bitches.'

Relief floods over me. I couldn't bear it if I lost my only friend.

'But mate,' you really need to grow a pair.'

As I let myself into the house, I can hear voices coming from the lounge. I close the front door quietly and stand in the hallway listening for a for a moment and try and identify who's here. The lounge door is suddenly flung widely open and Dad appears in front of me in a blast of warm air. I can feel the heat from the gas fire in the lounge so I know before Dad tells me that Auntie Bridget is here; the first thing she does on arrival is make Dad turn up the heating because she's always cold.

'There you are! Thought I heard you come in. Did you have a good day?'

'Fine.' I say. He doesn't mention the shrink so I don't either.

'Your uncle Ralph and Auntie Bridget are here.'

Hellos are called from the lounge. I follow Dad in and greet Uncle Ralph and Auntie Bridget with a kiss and a hug. A huge tray of doughnuts and a half empty box of muffins take up most of the coffee table. Uncle Ralph picks up the doughnut tray and offers me the last one.

'Want one love? I've saved you the best one.'

Cakes are Uncle Ralph's current fad; since he gave up smoking he's gone from boiled sweets to chocolate, a brief phase of peanuts (too hard on me teeth) and the current phase: cakes. I know that he's probably eaten most, if not all, of them yet he never puts on any weight.

I realise that I am hungry because thanks to Shana I never ate any lunch so I take the chocolate covered doughnut and take a huge bite.

'We were just talking about you,' Dad says as he settles himself back down onto the sofa. 'Come and sit down and hear what Uncle Ralph has to say.' He pats the seat next to him.

I settle down next to Dad and tuck into my doughnut and wait. I smell an ambush.

'I was just telling your Dad how I need some help at the office,' Uncle Ralph says in what he thinks is a casual way. Honestly, he's a worse actor than Dad, it sounds as if he's rehearsed those lines over and over.

My mouth full, I say nothing but raise my eyebrows.

'Yeah. Really need someone to help us catch up with all of the archiving, bleeding nightmare, it is.' Auntie Bridget flashes him a warning look for swearing but Uncle Ralph ignores her.

'Anyway,' he goes on. 'I was wondering if you could help me out? You'd be really doing me a favour. I'd pay you of course, Saturday mornings, nine 'til two suit you?'

I look at Dad who's intently scratching Skipper's ears and trying to pretend he's not listening.

'Would I be in the office on my own?'

'No, no, course not. I'll be there, and the printers, though you probably won't see much of them. Louise is coming in to help as well, she's sort of managing the archiving. Not my thing really, filing.'

'He's never away from the place, Josie.' Auntie Bridget pulls a face. 'It's as much as I can do to make him take Sundays off.'

Uncle Ralph gives her a look before carrying on. 'You come in for nine o'clock tomorrow morning. Your Dad says he'll drop you off.'

I bet he will. Dad is still pretending he's not listening, rubbing Skipper's tummy now, who's rolled onto his back to better enjoy all the attention.

I think about it for a few minutes, knowing that I don't really have a choice.

'Okay,' I say grudgingly.

'Brilliant!' says Dad with a beaming smile.

Auntie Bridget snorts. 'They're rubbish aren't they, pet? I don't know why they both do all of this pretending. Why can't they just be straight with you –

we're all worried about you and think that a bit of part-time work will do you good. Get you out of the house. Give you another interest.'

I can't help laughing, she's so right.

She turns to Ralph, 'How much are you going to pay her, Ralph?'

He looks shocked 'Well, I was thinking minimum wage...'

'Oh, no.' Auntie Bridget wags her cerise nailed finger at him. 'None of your cheapskate minimum wage nonsense. You pay her what you'd pay a temp – and I'll be checking that you do.'

Uncle Ralph doesn't look happy; he's notoriously tight and doesn't like parting with money. He doesn't see Auntie Bridget wink at me.

'Alright,' he says reluctantly. 'I'll suppose I'll have to pay the going rate.'

It appears I have a job.

Uncle Ralph and Auntie Bridget have left and Dad is frying chicken while I chop vegetables for a stir fry. Skipper is sitting expectantly at Dad's feet waiting for any scraps to come his way.

'Aren't you going to ask me?' I say.

'Ask what?'

'Auntie Bridget's right, you're rubbish at pretending.'

'Sorry. I'll try and be a bit more honest.' Dad turns round. 'Didn't know whether I should ask or not, you know, I don't want to pry. I don't expect you to tell me what you talked about or anything.'

'You can ask, doesn't mean I'll tell you.'

'But you did go to it?'

Dad knows me too well; he knows I only agreed to go to shut him up and that I probably wouldn't turn up.

I'm about to tell him how Mr Borden came and got me out of the lesson but then stop myself. He doesn't need to know that.

'Well for a start,' I say, 'the counsellor was a man. I thought you said it was a woman. I was expecting a woman. Not a man.'

'It should have been a woman.' Dad looks shocked. 'A Mrs Yvonne Fowler.'

'It was definitely a man.'

'I'm sorry. I can get it changed. I'll ring them first thing on Monday.'

'No, it's alright, don't bother, he's okay.' And as I say it, I realise that maybe it will be okay. Maybe it'll help to talk to someone, although obviously I can't tell him everything. But maybe I'll give it a try, see how it goes.

'Really?' Dad puts the spatula down and turns to look at me intently. 'Have you made another appointment?'

'Yeah. Next week.'

Dad's beaming again. 'That's great! I'm so pleased. Isn't that great, Skipper?' He beams down at Skipper who wags his tail.

'Dad?'

'Yeah?'

'Just don't expect too much, will you?'

Chapter 4
Josie

I woke up to the smell of burning bacon drifting up the stairs and the sound of Dad singing along to the radio at the top of his voice. He was so excited this morning, he tried to hide it but I could tell he was just so pleased that I'd agreed to take the job at Uncle Ralph's. He was bouncing around the kitchen, breadcrumbs and tomato ketchup flying everywhere, fat all over the cooker top; Mum would have gone mad if she was here. I persuaded him to put an apron on over his Dangermouse t-shirt – couldn't see it surviving all of the mess otherwise. Even Skipper seemed happier as he trotted around after Dad, his claws clicking on the tiles, even if it was because he could see some bacon scraps coming his way. As I sat down at the table, I looked at them both through the smoky fug coming off the frying pan and thought, if they can do it, so can I.

I couldn't get to sleep last night; the day's events kept running through my mind on a loop, but I made some decisions. Once I'd made my mind up about things I fell into a deep sleep and I didn't wake up until the alarm went off this morning.

Maybe it was the counselling that started me

thinking. I don't know, but I do know that I have to grow up and stop dwelling on the past and being so selfish. Because I have been selfish; imagining that I'm being all noble and protecting Dad from finding out the truth and that somehow I'm protecting Mum's memory. It's nearly a year since Mum died and it's very unlikely that the truth will come out after all this time (I keep telling myself this) and apart from *him* I'm the only one who knows about it and he's hardly likely to say anything now, is he?

I've wallowed long enough and I've decided that I have to get over things so I'm going to keep going to the counselling. Obviously, I can't tell him the truth about Mum but maybe he can help with other things. Like, the fact that I'm a complete weirdo and only have one friend in the whole world (obviously Dad and Skipper don't count).

Also, I'm going to try and *make an effort*, as Mum used to say. I could carry on moping around and being frightened of my own shadow or, to quote Biro, I can *grow a pair*. Time to wake up and get on with life, Mum dying must have been absolutely devastating for Dad and he tries really hard to be positive and get on with life so I'm going to try too.

The first effort I made was tucking into my bacon sandwich although I didn't really want it and, I even told Dad how tasty it was. I gave Skipper the burnt bits when Dad wasn't looking as I didn't want to hurt his feelings. I like my bacon well done but Dad had practically incinerated it and even Skipper had a job to choke it down.

And then I pasted a smile on my face and said I was looking forward to starting my new job and Dad was all pleased and gave me a big hug. And that made me feel better because I knew it cheered Dad up.

So I am trying.

Bit disappointed, if I'm honest. I was expecting a hustling, bustling newsroom, sort of like the Daily Planet in Superman. So the dusty, slightly grubby and scruffy office doesn't quite match up to Uncle Ralph's 'hold the front page' stories. Uncle Ralph told me to sit at someone called Ian's desk. As he's not here I've pushed all of his stuff out of the way and wiped it over with a damp cloth I found in the kitchen. The desk top was gross; sweet wrappers and crisp packets and, what looked like, pasty crumbs scattered everywhere. At least I hope that's what they were. I pulled one of the drawers open to look for a pen and hastily shut it again. Urgh, disgusting.

After that I made Uncle Ralph a cup of tea and looked out of the window. Louise is going 'to show me the ropes' when she arrives but she's not here yet.

'She'll be here soon, Josie,' Uncle Ralph calls over with a mouthful of doughnut. I think he's worried that I'll change my mind and go home.

The bang of the door downstairs interrupts the silence, so hopefully that's Louise. Seconds later the office door flies open and a fluffy dog with big floppy ears bounds through the door and heads straight for me. A woman follows behind him shouting loudly.

'Sprocket!' The dog ignores her and lollops around me like a giant puppy, ears flapping and his tail whirling around like helicopter blades. I reach down and stroke him and say hello and he rolls onto his back so I can rub his tummy.

'Sorry about him.' Louise comes over and hauls him up by grabbing his collar. 'I'm Louise, this is Sprocket and you must be Josie?'

'I am.'

'Nice to meet you, Josie, just ignore him.' She nods at Sprocket who's straining to get away from Louise and back to me and is half strangling himself. 'He'll stop eventually.'

'I don't mind,' I say, 'I like dogs.'

'Well, if you're sure,' she says and lets go of his collar.

Sprocket gets as close to me as he can and sits on my feet and gazes up at me with chocolate brown eyes and as I look down at him his tail starts to do the helicopter wag again.

I reach down and scratch his ears. 'It's okay, I'm used to dogs. He's lovely anyway.' I feel a pang of guilt; Skipper's been mostly ignored since Mum died, he was mainly her dog and at first we couldn't bear to look at him because he pined for her so much. Like us. He's like a ghost dog now, always there, desperate for a bit of attention and overjoyed with whatever scraps of affection come his way. I look at Sprocket gazing up at me and I feel suddenly choked. I make another resolution; make a big fuss of Skipper, he's grieving too.

'You okay?' Louise is looking at me with concern; I'm doing that staring thing again.

'Yeah, I'm fine.' I manage a smile.

'I'll just get a drink and I'll show you what we're doing.' Louise unravels her scarf and starts to unbutton her coat.

'That's okay,' I say. 'I'll make you a drink, the kettle's just boiled.'

'Oh, would you, that'd be lovely. White coffee, no sugar please.'

Sprocket follows me out to the kitchen and sits

immobile by my side while I make Louise's coffee; Skipper often does this so I know Sprocket's waiting for a biscuit. I'm in the process of searching the cupboards when Louise comes in.

'If you're looking for a biscuit you won't find them. I have to hide them.'

Louise laughs at the look on my face.

'I do. Your Uncle Ralph and Ian will scoff a whole packet with one cup of tea. I'll let you in on the secret if you promise not to tell them.'

She pulls out a drawer. 'Under the clean tea towels – there's no danger of them looking in there. Lucy and I are the only ones who know what a tea towel is for.' She puts her hand under the pile and pulls out a packet of custard creams.

Sprocket shuffles from foot to foot with his gaze fixed on the packet.

'Just one, that's all.' She takes one out of the packet and tosses it towards him and he snaps his jaws around it mid-air and swallows it in one gulp.

'Didn't touch the sides,' Louise laughs. 'Want one?' She offers me the packet.

'No, I'm alright thanks.'

'That's why you're lovely and slim,' she says as she crams a biscuit into her mouth. 'Me, no willpower at all.'

She takes another biscuit from the packet then tucks it back into the drawer under the tea towels.

'Right then, Josie, follow me and I'll initiate you in the wonderful ways of archiving. Be warned, you may need matchsticks to keep your eyes open, it's so boring.'

I try to look interested.

'Basically,' she says, 'You're going to be shredding a

load of old paper that goes back to the year dot.'

'Oh, okay.' I follow Louise to her desk.

'And the reason we have to do this is because your Uncle Ralph hasn't thrown anything out since he bought the place.'

'What?' Uncle Ralph looks up from his desk at the mention of his name.

'I was just telling Josie how you've never thrown anything away.'

'It's not that bad.'

'It is.' Louise bends down underneath her desk and drags a large cardboard box out and hoists it onto her desk. 'There's stuff in here so old it was done on a typewriter.'

By mid-morning there are three large black bin bags full of shredded paper and the shredder is so hot I think it might explode.

'Should probably have a break now or the shredder might give up the ghost entirely, better let it cool down for a while.' Louise looks as hot as I feel; I didn't know feeding old paper into a shredder could be so physical. I put a big jumper on this morning because it was cold outside but I'm regretting it now.

It's hardly exciting work but I've sort of enjoyed it, Louise is really nice and easy to get on with and I don't feel under scrutiny like I do at college. I don't feel like a weirdo.

'Is there a reason this dog is hanging around me?' Uncle Ralph shouts across the office. 'Because when I said you could bring it in, I didn't expect to have it sat on me.'

Sprocket isn't sitting on Uncle Ralph but he is sitting right beside him and looking at him expectantly. He can probably smell the stash of cakes and doughnuts in his desk.

'Stop exaggerating Ralph, he's not sitting on you and if it's that bad, I can go home.' Louise winks at me.

'I never said I minded, did I? Just saying, that's all.'

'I can go if he's a problem, I did tell you I had to bring him. He is my dog, can't expect someone else to look after him *all* the time. It is Saturday."

'No, it's all right, he's no bother.' Uncle Ralph pats Sprocket awkwardly on the head; he's worried now that he might not get the shredding done.

'Fancy a trip down to the precinct Josie? Leave this to cool down for a while and get a sandwich or something ready for lunchtime?

'Yes, I need to get something to eat. I'll get my coat.' I get my Parka from the back of Ian's chair and put it on and then think better of it and take it off. I'm far too hot and going outside will cool me down a bit. I feel quite brave going out without it; no hiding in the hood.

'Do you want anything Ralph?' Louise calls across to Uncle Ralph.

'I'll have a cheese and onion sarnie if they've got one.'

'Watch Sprocket for me. Won't be long.'

I head down the stairs and Louise follows but when we get to the bottom I stop and listen for a moment.

'What's that awful noise?'

Louise laughs. 'That'll be Sprocket. Howling.'

Uncle Ralph will *not* be happy.

The rest of the morning went really quickly; the shredder had cooled down when we got back and we resumed 'archiving'. Louise is really easy to get on with; I wish I could get on with people my own age as easily.

I don't feel like I'm being judged or that I have to analyse every word I say when I talk to her.

We don't talk about it but I know she's been through some tough times because Uncle Ralph told Dad and Dad told me. Apparently, Louise's Dad used to live next door to the Frogham Throttler and she nearly became a victim herself. Auntie Bridget always says that Uncle Ralph has no scruples but he didn't print a word about what happened to Louise until the trial. He could have had the scoop on the big newspapers but out of loyalty to Louise he didn't. Must have nearly killed him not printing it though.

And to think that it all happened just across the road from our house; unbelievable. I've racked my brains to see if I remember seeing Louise's Dad or the Frogham Throttler but I don't think I ever did. Even with my photographic memory.

'What have you got planned for the rest of the day, Josie? Anything exciting?'

'No, nothing, although my friend's asked me to go with him to audition musicians for his band, but I don't think I will.'

'Why not? Sounds like fun, you might meet a hunky bass player, or have you already got a boyfriend?'

Me? Got a boyfriend? Fat chance. Although I'm flattered that Louise thinks it's even a possibility.

'No, I'm not seeing anyone at the moment.' And never have done.

'What're they called? This band?'

'Tourists of Reality.'

'Really?'

'I know. Cringe.'

Louise laughs. 'Yeah, a bit. But if you analyse a lot of the names they're cringe, until they make it big.'

'Tourists of Reality are not going to make it big. Trust me.'

'How can you be so sure?'

'Because Biro can't sing. At all.'

Sounds really disloyal saying it out loud and I suddenly feel crap. I only have one friend and I've just slagged him off.

'What time did you say the auditions start?'

'Two o'clock.'

We're waiting in one of the college music rooms for the would-be band members to arrive. I felt compelled to come and support Biro, mostly because I need to make it up to him after slagging him off to Louise. Although obviously I won't tell him that I did. Ever.

'It's only quarter past. No one's ever on time.'

'True.' Biro looks at his watch again. 'I'll just go and check the main door, make sure there's no one out there waiting 'cos they don't know where to go.'

I huddle into my Parka and wrap my arms around myself. It's cold in here, the heating must have been turned off for the weekend. There aren't any windows in the room and the walls are made of some strange wood stuff with holes in it. Sound proofing, according to Biro. It doesn't look like anyone is going to turn up and although I feel sorry for Biro, selfishly, I'll be happy to just go home.

The door is flung open and an overweight boy with greasy, mousey, shoulder length hair is almost pushed into the room by Biro.

'Hey, look who was outside! Josie, meet Mogs. He plays bass guitar.'

Mogs puts a hand up and says what I think is *hi* but I can't be sure as he mumbles it through a curtain of hair.

'No one else out there?'

'No, not yet.'

''Scoming,' says Mogs.

'Sorry?'

'Danny's coming.' He hooks his fingers around his hair and parts it to reveal a pale, pudgy face with a porridge like complexion.

He's gonna be a bit late 'cos he's got to get the keyboard from his sister's house.'

'Cool,' says Biro, brightening up.

'Yeah. She said he could borrow it as long as she gets it back before Monday 'cos she needs it for her singalong night at the old people's home.'

I find that I can't look at Biro; it's not exactly hard rock is it?

'Okay, do you want to show me what you can do? Might as well make a start.'

Mogs shrugs. 'Kay. You say you'd got an amp?'

'Yeah.'

Mogs unzips his guitar from the case and lays it reverently on the floor, he then unzips his duffel coat to reveal a faded Metallica t-shirt.

I watch as he plugs the guitar into the amp and passes a webbed strap over his shoulder and picks the guitar up and clips it on.

'So, what do you want me to play?'

'What sort of stuff do you normally play?'

Well.' Mogs sniffs from behind his hair. 'Y'know, the classics.'

Biro looks horrified. 'What? Classical music?'

Mogs peers out from between his hair-curtain and gives Biro a puzzled look. 'Floyd, Purple, bit of modern, y'know, Muse, Imagine Dragons.'

'Oh yeah, course.' Biro looks embarrassed. 'Give us

what you got then, man.'

Did he really say man? This is going to be much, much worse than I thought. I step backwards and slide down the wall and settle myself on the floor. I get ready to stick my fingers in my ears.

Mogs frowns in concentration, and through the gap in his hair I can see the blood rush to the acne on his face as he starts to play. I quietly slide my hands up to cover my ears but then stop as they reach my chin.

He's actually pretty good.

I put my hands down and watch. As Mogs plays, a transformation comes over him, his fingers fly over the strings and he relaxes and seems to forget we're even here.

Biro and I look at each other, our mouths hanging open in amazement and as Mogs finishes a beaming smile appears on Biro's face.

'That was something else, man. Amazing, can't beat a bit of Floyd'.

I have to agree, it was absolutely amazing and I know nothing about Floyd, whoever he is.

Mogs doesn't speak, just nods, but he does have a beaming smile on his face.

'So I guess I've found my bass player – if you want in?'

'Yeah.' Mogs nods some more. 'I'm in.'

The clank of the door opening interrupts us and a tall figure hidden by an enormous keyboard pushes his way into the room.

'Hey, is this the right place for the band auditions?'

'It is, mate.' Biro grabs hold of the end of the keyboard and they manhandle it onto the floor and the tall figure straightens up.

'Couldn't carry the stand so it'll have to go on a

couple of chairs or something. I'm Danny by the way.'

He stands and looks around at us all and smiles. Danny is the opposite of Mogs; tall, clear skinned, blonde and very good looking. I pull my hood down further over my face and wrap my arms around my legs again.

Yeah, I know I'm supposed to have turned over a new leaf but give me time.

'Hi, Danny. I'm Biro, this is Josie and you know Mogs?' Danny beams around at me and Mogs.

'Yeah, we were at school together.' Danny drags two chairs over next to Mogs and lays the keyboard across them and then hunts around for a socket, finds one and plugs in the keyboard.

'Okay,' he says kneeling down in front of the keyboard, 'What do you want me to play?'

'Anything you like,' says Biro.

Danny pulls a crumpled piece of paper out of his pocket and carefully smooths it out with his hands. 'Glad you said that 'cos I only brought one song with me.' He props the paper up against the chair back in front of the keyboard.

'You need to read the music?' Biro looks horrified.

'Yeah 'cos I haven't been playing that long – is it a problem?'

'No, no problem,' Biro says unconvincingly. 'Let's hear it, man.'

Danny frowns in concentration and slowly starts to play and the only way to describe it is painful. I can't play any instruments at all but I honestly think I could do a better job than him. I can't even make out what tune it is and every so often Danny pauses, scrutinises the keyboard to find the right key and then starts playing again.

47

Make it stop. Please.

'That's great, thanks.' Biro holds his hand up. 'You've not been in a band before?'

'Yeah, was in Stereo Outcast for a while.'

'Playing keyboard?'

'No.' Danny looks embarrassed. 'They gave me a guitar and said just to pretend I was playing it.'

I've seen Stereo Outcast; they're always auditioning for X Factor type shows and probably spend more time doing their hair than practising playing.

'Then they found someone who could really play, so I left.'

'To be fair you only need to know a few chords, you wouldn't be playing the whole thing. Just a bit of backing.'

Danny perks up. 'Yeah?'

'Yeah. I can teach you the chords – do you want in?'

'Defo.'

A lot of whooping and fist bumping goes on and I sit quietly watching. Biro's no fool and I can see the way his mind is working, Danny's going to be the eye candy of the band, the one to draw the girls in.

'Josie!'

'What?'

'You're in too.'

'Me? I can't play anything, or sing.'

Biro comes over and drags me to my feet and puts his arm around my shoulders.

'Dudes, meet your band manager.'

Chapter 5

Josie

I got a text yesterday from Adam. For a minute I didn't have a clue who it was texting me. I don't have any boys' phone numbers on my phone. In fact, I don't have many numbers on my phone at all and the only texts I get are from Biro and they're usually only a few words, like *cu at 12* or *coming 2 mine*? And I didn't even give Adam my number so he must have got it from my college file. Anyway, I saw this text from an unknown number and I opened it and there's this great long message saying that he hoped I wanted to continue the counselling and he thinks that it would be beneficial if I have two sessions a week. Tuesdays and Fridays.

Initially, it was a no from me and I was annoyed because I felt I was being pressured by him and I didn't like it that he'd texted me. But then I thought about it for a while and decided that maybe I was overreacting. And then I thought well if I have double the sessions it'll be over that much quicker won't it? It'll take half the time. I also need to keep positive and try to be more, oh I don't know, just more. So I texted back *ok*. I then spent the next hour agonising that I should have said more in the message and that just one word was a bit rude and pathetic.

Got myself in a right state about it and was just about to spiral down into a complete case of self-loathing when Adam texted again with *great* and a smiley face and that made me feel better.

See, the state I got in over that shows that I definitely need counselling. This is also why I don't do *any* social media. I'd waste so much time worrying about it I'd never be able to leave the house.

I didn't have to be dragged out of a tutorial this time, I was all grown up and left five minutes before my appointment so I'd get there just right; not so early that I'd look desperate and not late so that I look immature and childish and as if I'm trying to make a point. But as it turned out was there late because it took me forever to find the counselling room. I got lost a couple of times because I followed Adam here last time so I didn't take any notice of where I was going. I was just about to give up and go to the student office to ask someone for directions when I turned a corner and there it was.

We sit in the same places as last time and his legs are just as long and his knees are still nearly touching mine but I am trying not to flinch away and get all precious about personal space. I stopped myself from putting my hood up to hide in so am feeling pretty pleased with myself although I do still have my Parka on. One step at a time.

He gave me a lovely smile and looked pleased to see me when I arrived (although obviously he does that to everyone) but he's very good at his job and he did make me feel welcome. I apologised for being late and told him how I got lost and nearly had to go to the student office but he didn't say anything so I thought that maybe I was gabbling too much so I shut up. Then it went all quiet. The silence was just starting to feel uncomfortable when he started talking.

'How have you been since we last talked, Josie?'

'Okay.'

'Have you had any thoughts on what you'd like to talk about?'

I shrug. I have no idea what to say. I'm hoping he'll just ask questions and I can answer them and that'll be that.

He rubs his jaw with his hands and looks thoughtful.

'Okay. Perhaps it'll help if I tell you a bit about myself.'

Good, better him talking than me. And it'll take up a good bit of the session time.

'I was born and brought up in Frogham, actually attended this college! And I didn't start off wanting to be a counsellor at all I just wanted to make lots of money. So I worked in marketing for a while and I was pretty good at it and I started to make decent money. But then I realised that something was missing, that what I was doing didn't mean anything to me, that I wanted something more, something more than just making money. I wanted to do something that *mattered*.'

I stifle a yawn. So far, so predictable.

'Because I'd had counselling myself, you know. It was a long time ago but I found that it definitely helped.'

I look at him in surprise, what could he possibly need counselling for?

'Does that surprise you?' Adam laughs. 'Appearances can be deceptive, people, especially men, are very good are hiding their feelings. Everyone has their own problems and issues and everyone needs help sometimes.'

'Why did you have counselling?' Is it rude to ask? Probably, but if he didn't want to talk about it, he surely wouldn't have told me.

'My mother had died. Suddenly. And I wasn't coping very well.'

'Oh.'

'So I do have some idea of what you're going through, Josie. I was the same age as you although,' he pauses, 'You're much more mature than I was.'

I look at him, I don't know what to say. At last, someone who understands how I feel.

Mature, he called me mature.

'Although, like you,' he goes on, 'I didn't see how it could possibly help, just talking to someone, but it did. Although it took quite a while.'

We sit in silence for a few moments and I try to imagine Adam at seventeen. I bet he'd have been just as good looking, one of the popular ones. I wouldn't have merited a second glance from him. He clears his throat and for a minute I have the feeling that he knows exactly what I'm thinking and I feel a blush creep up my face.

'So. Now that you know a bit about me, how about we start over?' He smiles and his eyes crinkle up at the corners and look all twinkly. 'So, talk to me.'

He looks so approachable and the thought crosses my mind: maybe this won't be so bad after all.

'What time?'

'You'll be third on, second from last.'

'Wow, that's like, amazing, how did you even manage that? It's impossible to get a gig there, people are queuing up to get in.' Biro looks at me in total awe and I bask in the warmth of the compliment.

It is pretty amazing; Tourists of Reality are booked to play at the Old Vic's weekly band night in a couple of weeks' time. It was worrying me, this band manager thing. I don't like to take anything on – although, technically, I was forced into it - and not do it properly but I couldn't see what I could do, I know nothing about bands, promotion, anything. Biro couldn't have picked a worse person to be band manager.

I could have just said I wouldn't do it, and if it had been last week, I would have done that even though I know Biro would have been disappointed and hurt. But I thought, no, it's a new me now so get on with it. But it's all very well thinking positively but I hadn't a clue what to do. So there I was, looking miserable, and Dad asked me what was wrong so instead of bottling it up and moping I told him.

'Manager?' he'd said in disbelief and I nearly burst into tears. I knew I was going to let everyone down.

Typical Dad, he started coming up with ideas, trying to put everything right like he always does, bless him. He suggested playing at the George but I knew Biro wouldn't do it because I'd already asked him, he doesn't want his Dad letting him play there as a favour.

'Nepotism.' he'd said when I suggested it, but I think it's more because the George is definitely not cool. And he didn't want his Dad joining in and taking over.

Anyway, turns out that Dad knows the landlord of the Old Vic, they played football for the same team back in the day and they still keep in touch. Before I knew it, Dad was on the phone to him and after a bit of banter and reminiscing from Dad, Tourists of Reality were booked to play there two weeks on Friday.

'You done good, Josie, I don't know how but you done good.' Biro is shaking his head in disbelief.

I sit back and bask a bit more.

Not lying, am I? Just not saying anything. He doesn't need to know that I've never actually been in the Old Vic or even know where it is. I'd never even heard of the Old Vic before Dad told me about it. Had no idea they did a band night or that it was *the* place to play, not that Tourists of Reality will be paid or anything but apparently bands would kill for an unpaid Friday night spot there. Dad says he'll take me in there before band night so I don't look a complete idiot on the night.

I thought it was weird it being in a pub because we're not even old enough to drink but Dad says it's fine, band night has been going for years and the landlord can spot an underage drinker a mile off. Dad says he's really strict because he doesn't want to lose his licence and if we try to buy alcohol we'll be out on our ear.

'We'd better start practising, decide what we're going to play in our set. Have to get the guys together.'

'Who's playing what?' says a whiny voice.

I look up; We're at a tucked away table at the back of the canteen but the Clackers have found us. Shana can sniff out the merest hint of gossip from a mile away.

She slides into the chair next to Biro and a blast of her sweet fruity bubble gum drifts across the table. Stacey sits down next to me but doesn't acknowledge me as she's too busy watching Shana. Ellie hovers at the end of the table holding her lunch tray, unsure what to do as there aren't any more chairs. Shana and Stacey ignore her. Ellie looks at both of them then bangs the tray down onto the table and walks off.

'Nothing you'd be interested in,' Biro says loftily.

'Is that right, Josie?' Shana looks straight at me, gum

clacking. Does she eat with that in her mouth? Course not, she never eats, just buys a salad and pushes it around the plate. Probably hasn't eaten a meal since year eleven.

I shrug, unsure what to say.

'You've got me interested now, being so mysterious.' Clack, clack. The smell of strawberry bubble gum drifts over every time she speaks.

'Me too,' whines Stacey. Clack clack.

Ellie comes back dragging a chair and squashes it onto the end of the table between Shana and Stacey and sits down.

'Hey, fattie, leave me a bit of space,' Shana squeals, moving her tray an inch away from Ellie with exaggerated arm movements.

Stacey giggles. 'Fattie! You're like, *so* funny Shana.'

Ellie's face flushes and her lips tighten, she's not fat at all but she's always been self-conscious about her legs. She puts her head down and stares intently at her food.

'Only joking, babes.' Shana puts one manicured finger on Ellie's hand. 'I'm not fat shaming you, I don't think you're fat no matter what anyone else says.'

Ellie stares fixedly down at her food and her face goes even redder.

'So, Stefan.' Shana turns and directs the full force of her eye fluttering attention at Biro. She doesn't fancy him in the slightest but she can't help herself. 'What are you practising and where are you playing?'

Biro takes a slurp of his drink, gazes straight at me and ignores her.

'Biro's band is playing at the Vic,' I blurt out. She won't give up until she knows, so we might as well get it over with.

'What? Didn't know you even had a band, you kept that a big secret. Aren't the Vic a bit fussy over who they let play?'

Biro drains the rest of his drink loudly through the straw and bangs it down on the table.

'Yeah, they are fussy, that's why we're playing. Two weeks on Friday if you want to come and see us. Tourists of Reality,' he says loudly unable to stop himself bragging.

'Ooh,' squeals Shana. 'How exciting, might just do that. Are you in the band, Josie?'

Stacey bursts out laughing and Shana joins in. I sneak a look at Ellie, she's still concentrating on her food although I notice she hasn't eaten anything.

'No, she's not in the band,' says Biro loudly. 'She's the manager.'

I copy Ellie and stare at my food.

Great. Now the whole world will know.

I lie in bed and think through the events of the day. Skipper is snuggled up next to me snoring gently. He was waiting as usual when I got home; standing in the lounge doorway staring at the front door. I knelt down and ruffled his ears and talked to him and I thought he was going to go into orbit his stumpy little tail wagged so hard.

He's pretty much followed me around the house since then so I let him into my room while I got ready for bed and he's still here. There's something comforting about his warm, furry little body and I don't mind if he sleeps on my bed. I quite like it really.

Thinking back, it's been a good day; Biro thinks I'm pretty cool for getting him a gig at the Vic - even if it was Dad that did it really. On the downside I'm feeling nervous about what Tourists of Reality are going to be like seeing as they've never even played a gig together. Visions of Danny plonking along on the keyboard and Biro's awful voice make me break out in a cold sweat, especially with the Clackers coming to watch. They were nearly hysterical with laughter at the thought of me being the band manager. Shana asked Biro if they would rather have had someone who, like, talks to people. Nice. So they're going to be completely brutal about Tourists of Reality if they think they're crap and I'll be for it as well.

I can hear the sniggering and laughing at college already and they haven't even played yet. I'm just praying that Danny's good looks and Mogs's amazing guitar playing will counteract the bad bits. If only the Clackers weren't coming; I know they'll make it their mission to be there because as well as gossip Shana can smell a disaster a mile away. So barring illness or death, they'll be watching. Maybe I could poison her. Make her eat a doughnut, that'd probably do it.

Nothing I can do about it really though is there? So grow a pair, as Biro says. It's not like I have to get up and perform and Biro and the others don't seem bothered at all. Just shows that I'm not normal – no one else worries about what people think about them like I do. Man up. Or woman up. Girl up even.

I think the counselling with Adam is helping, I can definitely feel that even after two sessions. He's been through it, losing his mum, so he knows how I feel and I feel quite special that he felt able to share that with me. When he talked about his mum his face looked all sad and vulnerable and his voice went a bit funny. We talked about his mum quite a lot; she died suddenly of a heart attack from an undiagnosed heart condition and to make things worse Adam had to be tested for the same defect. Turns out he's fine but that must have been awful on top of her dying. He actually talked about it to me and it made me feel better because I felt I helped him in a strange sort of way, even though he's counselling me. But it doesn't feel like counselling, feels more like talking to a friend.

Poor Adam, at least I have Dad, Adam said that his dad was more interested in finding himself a new wife than worrying about him, said his dad pretty much abandoned him.

I did tell him a little bit about Mum, about how we used to do things together and how she always totally understood me like no one else does, not even Dad, bless him. And I am angry with her for dying, which is really stupid, I know. It's not as if she had a choice but I do feel sort of abandoned too.

Adam. He's so nice and he really listened, properly listened.

Of course, I couldn't be totally honest with him because that would be betraying Mum and I can't do that. Even though Adam can't tell anyone what we talk about because it's all totally confidential I can't take the risk of Dad ever finding out because that would ruin everything, forever. He'd never think the same about Mum again and I can't have that, I can't have Mum's memory ruined for a stupid mistake which I know if she was still alive, she'd have put right. I know she would.

I can live with it and not tell anyone and eventually it'll be like it never happened.

But I just wish I hadn't found out.

I wish I didn't know that Mum was having an affair.

Chapter 6

Robbie

I know she's only been to a few sessions but I can definitely see a difference in Josie since she started the counselling. The very fact that she's going at all is a massive step forward. I honestly thought she'd point blank refuse to go. I'm keep everything crossed at the moment that she keeps going because she seems so much more positive and willing to try things and that's got to help her to get over losing her mum.

I think the job at the newspaper is helping too. I've had a word on the quiet with Ralph and he says she's settling in really well even though she's only been there for a couple of Saturdays. Apparently, she gets on really well with Louise even though there's a big age difference and Ralph says she's coming out of herself a bit. Maybe it's because Louise is about the same age as Nessa, sort of a mother figure. Although to be honest it hurts to even think like that; feels as if I'm being disloyal to my Nessa.

I only rang Ralph for a quick chat but I had a job to get him off the phone because he started prattling on about some dog that was howling and how they were taking advantage of him and I thought, here we go, another Ralph rant, so I said there was someone at the door and I put the phone down. Don't think he was very happy. I know he's my brother and everything but sometimes I've got a job to shut him up. He's like a dog with a bone, on and on and on. Mind you, I don't know what I'd have done without him this last year; he's been a diamond, an absolute diamond.

It was an even bigger shock when Josie came home and told me that Biro had made her the manager of his band. Didn't even know he had a band – it's called Tourists are Salty or something like that, some contrived arty-farty name. I was absolutely gobsmacked – Josie, a manager? She's near genius clever and can do pretty much anything but manage a band? I don't know what Biro was thinking and I didn't want to hurt her feelings and I'd certainly never say it, but our Josie's not manager material; too shy and reserved, not the pushy type at all.

Maybe it'll bring her out of herself a bit, give her a bit of confidence, I hope so. Luckily, I don't think Josie noticed how surprised I was about it, I managed to cover it up well.

'What do managers do?' she asked.

'Manage,' I said. 'Get the band out there, get them known, get them places to play at and most importantly, get them a following. Because without a following you might as well not bother because even if you get them gigs no one will bother coming to see them.'

I could see the panic on her face and I racked my brains to think how I could help her. Then I remembered that I used to play in a Sunday football team with Jason who runs the Old Vic pub. We go back years to when we first moved to Frogham and he owes me a few favours so I called one of them in. When I knew him, he was a skinny lad who used to run up and down that pitch like a rocket. That was a few years ago and now he runs the pub he obviously drinks a lot of the profits because I shouldn't think he'd be fit enough to walk the length of the pitch with the size of the beer gut on him. But the Old Vic have all the up and coming bands play there and some of the ones on the way down and it's got itself a name as the place to watch live music. Just the place for Biro's band to play.

Jason wasn't at all keen when I asked him, says he's got his reputation to think of and can't be just having any old rubbish playing in his gaff. So, I had to do a bit of arm twisting and give him a gentle reminder about how I helped him with his tax returns a few times when he was looking at a fine because he'd made such a mess of it. He ummed and aahed but gave in eventually and agreed to put them on the bill in a couple of weeks' time. I just hope they're not complete shite or else I'll never hear the end of it from him. Most likely I'll have to do Jason's next tax return for free but that's a small price to pay to put a smile on Josie's face. And I'm not proud of it but I did play the grieving widower card as well, felt a bit bad about that but it's for a good cause.

I did think about sneaking in and watching this band to see what they're like. I do like a bit of live music and I know Biro is a clever lad, plays the guitar, piano, the lot. And he's the singer too. I might pop in and watch them, the Vic's a dark and dingy old boozer so they won't notice me in the corner. Keep a sneaky eye on Josie, too; she'll never even know I'm there. Not because I think she'd do anything wrong, I know she wouldn't, she's not like that. No, it's everyone else that bothers me; Josie's so young and trusting, a real innocent.

Although I'm not sure if I should; part of me thinks that'd be like spying on her and I shouldn't do it but the other part of me just wants to protect her.

I'll have to give it some thought.

Makes it easier for me though, knowing that Josie is trying to move on, like I'm trying to. Because I still have dark days although I try my best to hide them. I miss Nessa so much and I can't believe she's gone and most mornings when I wake up, for a moment I feel quite happy and then reality crashes in and I remember she's dead. It catches me unawares; I'll see something or someone will say something funny and I think, I'll tell Nessa when I get home and then a split second later, I remember she's not there. It'll be a year ago next month, a whole year. It seems like only yesterday and forever ago.

Chapter 7

Josie

Biro has managed to borrow one of the music rooms again for the band's first rehearsal. It's much bigger than the one we did the auditions in but this time we're not allowed to let ourselves in. For some reason the caretaker has to let us in and he says he'll be back to lock up afterwards. Biro is fuming and doesn't know why we can't just turn up like we did before and lock up when we leave. Caretaker Jeff informs us that it's because it's a Saturday. It was a Saturday before, Biro tells him, but this argument doesn't seem to make any difference to Jeff. Caretaker Jeff is old, at least as old as Dad, miserable (not like Dad) and awkward.

He makes a big deal of unlocking the music room door after taking forever to find the right key from a great big jangly bunch, and then he won't let us touch anything until he's given us a health and safety lecture on the correct way to move furniture.

'If you want to move the tables and chairs you have to put them back exactly where they were when you've finished. I suggest you take a photo on your phone to make sure you return them to the correct position. I'll be back in three hours to lock up and inspect the room.'

Hopefully he'll go now. But he doesn't, he stands there with his arms folded and feet apart, blocking the doorway. I don't know what we're supposed to say and I can hear the sound of Danny and Mogs' voices and footsteps coming down the corridor.

'Just give us the keys and we'll lock up, drop 'em off to you on the way out.' Biro looks down at Jeff with a *leave now* glare.

'Oh, no, no, no.' Jeff shakes his head. 'More than my job's worth to do that. No, I'll be back in three hours.'

He stands there, feet planted firmly apart like we're going to try and knock him over. What's he waiting for?

'For fuck's sake,' Biro mutters under his breath.

'What was that?' Jeff looks at Biro suspiciously.

'I was just saying, you can bob off now, Jeff. We're good, we know how to move the tables and stuff.' I look at Biro and recognise the signs; he's ready to explode.

'Bob off?' Jeff says. 'Bob off? I'll decide when I bob off, son. I don't know who you think you're talking to, you cocky little sod.'

OMG. I can see that we're not going to be rehearsing today, at least not in this room. Biro will not back down; he never does. Might as well zip my coat back up.

Before Biro can respond Danny and Mogs appear behind Jeff and he reluctantly moves aside ever so slightly and lets them squeeze past him to come into the room.

Jeff looks Mogs and Danny up and down with a frown.

'Hello,' says Danny pleasantly. 'I was just saying to Mogs what a brilliant job someone has made of those new waste bins in the cafeteria. Was that your idea by any chance?'

Jeff looks taken aback for a moment but soon recovers his composure. He preens and looks proud. 'It was. Took a bit of doing but I persuaded the canteen staff in the end. Much tidier.'

'Cracking job,' says Danny.

The canteen has a new system for leftover scraps from the plates; instead of flinging it in the bin by the door as you walk out, the bins have been moved to the back of the hall by the fire exit. Everyone's moaning about what a stupid idea it is as you have to make a detour right around the hall. Nobody can understand why it was changed as it was perfectly alright as it was. After a couple of days some bright spark left a Tesco's carrier bag hanging on the exit door's handle and now everyone has started scaping their plates into that instead.

Mogs and Biro go straight over to the desks and start moving them and I cross my fingers that Jeff doesn't insist on giving them the health and safety lecture. Biro stands and watches them with ears that are so red I'm surprised there's not steam coming out of them.

'Well,' says Jeff, still preening from Danny's compliment. 'I'll leave you to it. Be back at nine.' He plods off down the corridor and I close the door firmly behind him.

'Miserable old fucker,' Biro says.

Danny and I look at each other; Biro in a bad mood is not a pleasant sight.

'You defused it well,' I say to Danny. 'How did you know it was him who did the bins?'

Danny laughs. 'My auntie's a cook in the canteen.

They all want to kill him for his stupid idea. They're swapping the bins back on Monday.'

'I'd like to see his face when they do.'

'Are we here to rehearse or to talk about sad old bastards?' Biro shouts at us. 'Because we're wasting practice time.'

'Okay, I'll get the keyboard set up,' Danny says with a smile as he pulls the keyboard out of the bag and puts it on a desk. A bit of an improvement on using two chairs, at least he won't have to kneel down to play it. Luckily Biro's bad mood doesn't seem to affect Danny or Mogs who's totally engrossed in tuning his guitar. Good job too as there's only room for one diva in this room.

'You'll defo have the legs for that when we play at the Vic?' Biro frowns at Danny.

'Yeah.' Danny plugs the cable into the wall socket. 'As long as I can get a lift. If I have to get the bus, I won't be able to carry them as well as the keyboard.'

The legs are obviously bothering Biro; a keyboard on two chairs isn't going to look cool.

'My Dad can pick you up,' I surprise myself by saying. 'He'll be dropping me off anyway so he won't mind.' Dad won't mind at all; he'd drive round and pick everyone up if I asked him to.

Danny smiles his megawatt smile.

'Oh, thanks, Jose, that'd be great.'

Danny has the longest eyelashes I've ever seen, and that includes on any girl I know. He seems so nice too, so easy to get along with. Normally I can't even look at anyone as good looking as Danny, let alone talk to them but he's so nice. As long as there are lots of girls in the audience it won't matter how bad his playing is as they'll be too busy drooling over him.

We push the rest of the tables up against one wall and stack the chairs in the corner.

'Okay, that'll do.' Biro pulls a bunch of papers out of his pocket. 'This is the playlist. I've put ten songs on it in order of play but obviously we won't get to play them all, but better to have too many than not enough.'

'Cool.' Mogs gives the list a cursory look and then scrunches it up and puts it in his pocket.

Danny looks a bit unsure. 'Are we going to have the music to follow?' He looks at Mogs then Biro. 'Only I don't know these songs.'

Mogs looks surprised. 'Just improvise, won't we?'

'Yeah, sure. Look Danny, I'll show you a few chords and you just play the same chords in a different key. Just follow us, play a few chords as and when.'

'Oh.' Danny looks even more unsure.

'Don't worry mate, it'll be a breeze.'

Biro spends the next hour showing Danny the keys; it's pretty straightforward and Danny perks up when he realises that he doesn't have to play the whole song. Mogs sits on the floor in the corner with his earbuds in and his eyes closed listening to music.

I'm feeling bored and wishing I hadn't come and the plink plonk of the keyboard is starting to get on my nerves.

'Okay, Mogs, MOGS!'

Mogs looks up with sleepy eyes.

'We're going to start, Danny's got the hang of the chords so we'll go through the list straight from the top.

'Kay, dude.' Mogs pulls himself up off the floor and picks his guitar up from the table.

'Don't you want to check the list, Mogs? Check what we're playing?' Biro asks.

Mogs blinks at Biro through his hair and shakes his

head.

'No.'

Biro doesn't look very impressed and I hope for Mogs' sake that he remembers the order otherwise Biro will definitely go into orbit.

Danny stands expectantly at the keyboard, Mogs passes the guitar strap over his shoulder and his fingers hover over the keys. Biro picks up his guitar and adjusts the microphone so it's just slightly too high and he looks all lead singerish trying to reach it.

'One, two, three!' Biro shouts.

An hour and a half later and I think we've established that:
   a. Mogs is an even better guitar player than we thought – he can play *anything*. Without music. And he remembered the running order perfectly.
   b. Biro cannot sing.
   c. Danny has absolutely no rhythm. At all.
   d. After the gig at the Vic I will need to leave college and possibly Frogham and get a job as I won't be able to cope with the humiliation and embarrassment. What I said about no one noticing that Danny can't play – I was wrong.

'No, mate, no. It's quick, quick, slow, slow, then on the next bar it's quick, quick, and just one slow.' Biro is speaking very slowly and calmly but he doesn't fool me, I can see his left eye twitching; a sure sign that he's had enough.

'Yep, got that.' Danny smiles. 'But remind me, what's a bar again?'

Biro sits down on the desk next to Danny and puts his head in his hands.

'You alright, Biro?' Danny looks at Biro with concern.

Biro doesn't speak for a while and the room becomes very quiet. I pull my Parka hood up and pull the woolly bit down over my eyes. Yeah, I know I said I wasn't going to do that anymore but I know what's coming and I really feel for Danny. Mogs coughs nervously and finds his fingernails suddenly fascinating. He has his head bent right over so his hair covers his entire face.

'The thing is, mate...' Biro starts to say to Danny.

Danny looks at Biro expectantly.

'Well, the thing is, um...'

Danny waits.

'I don't think this is working out mate, the keyboard thing. You know, maybe you should practice a bit more, have a few lessons before you think about joining a band.'

Danny's face drops.

'I'm crap, aren't I?' he says. 'It's Stereo Outcast all over again.'

'Sorry, mate.'

Danny perks up. 'What if I pretend to play guitar like I did in Stereo Outcast? That could work.'

'We need a keyboard player,' says Biro.

'You could play keyboards,' Danny says. 'Mogs plays enough guitar for two people.'

This is true; Biro can play well but Mogs leaves him standing.

'Hmm. Dunno.'

I watch Biro thinking it over, he probably realises that the chances of getting anyone else to join the band are non-existent. Without another band member we can kiss goodbye to the gig at the Old Vic.

'Okay we'll give it a try. See if it works.' Biro gives Danny his guitar and unplugs it from the amp.

'We'll run through the first number and if it looks like a goer, we'll swap the microphone onto the keyboard and put you up the back between me and Mogs.'

Danny nods and puts the strap over his shoulder and positions his hands on the guitar so it looks like he's playing.

'Right,' says Biro, 'one, two, three...'

Mogs starts to play the opening bars and Biro joins in on the keyboard. Danny pretends to play the guitar and looks pretty convincing to me. Unless anyone's looking for it, they wouldn't know.

This could work.

Biro opens his mouth to sing.

Or maybe not.

Biro's horrible wail fills the room but doesn't sound as awful as usual because Danny is also belting out the opening bars and his voice somehow dilutes the awfulness of Biro.

They sing the whole of the first song and I pull my hood back off my head so I can hear properly.

Admittedly, Danny is singing a lot of the words wrong but the voice, the voice is not bad, much better than Biro's.

Mogs finishes and stands staring, his fingers still, watching Danny in surprise. Biro stares at Danny, frowning.

Danny realises that we're all staring at him.

'Sorry, wasn't I supposed to sing?'

'Mate, why didn't you tell us you could sing?'

Danny shrugs. 'You never asked.'

'How is it,' ask Mogs with a puzzled expression on

his face, 'That you have no timing at all on the keyboard but you can sing in time? And in tune?'

'Yeah, he's got a point, dude, how does that work?'

'Dunno.' Danny shrugs again. 'I think it's my ear, eye and hand co-ordination or something like that. When I sing, well, I just sing.'

'That was epic, dude.' Biro shakes his head in disbelief. 'Epic.'

'Thanks.' Danny looks worried again. 'But I'm not great at the words, if I can't remember them, I sort of just make them up.'

'Not a problem, dude. No one listens to the words anyway.' Biro comes out from behind the keyboard and claps an arm around Danny's shoulder. 'Now. What I think we'll do, is run through all the numbers on the sheet with both of us singing, see how it goes.'

'Okay, Biro.' Danny starts to take off Biro's guitar. 'No, no, leave it on, mate, it looks good. I reckon I'll be centre stage and you and Mogs can be either side of me. What do you reckon, Josie?'

'Good idea,' I agree.

Biro resumes his position behind the keyboard.

'From the top, dudes.'

Tourists of Reality have arrived.

Chapter 8

Josie

I'm a bit early. Does that look really sad? It probably does. Who in their right mind gets to a counselling session early? But it doesn't feel like counselling, it's more like talking to a good friend.

I feel safe with Adam.

I've decided I'm not going to feel bad about how I feel; I usually manage to make myself feel guilty about everything. This counselling is helping me and that's all that matters.

The door's open so I go in and take my coat off and sling it over the back of the chair, settle down in the seat and wait for Adam to arrive.

Yes. I've taken my coat off; no more huddling and hiding in my Parka. It's a new development, the taking off of the coat. Not a major deal for most people but for me it's a massive step forward. Not saying that I'm that brave anywhere else, apart from Uncle Ralph's office, but one step at a time. I hope the day is not too far away when I can sit in the college canteen without huddling and hiding in my Parka. I'm a good advert for this counselling – only my fifth session and it's already made such a difference. Obviously, I've still got a long way to go but I'm on my way and I'm feeling a bit better every day. There are still some things that I haven't talked about, and one thing that I'll never talk about, but I'm getting there.

I'm impatient for Adam to arrive so we can get started; I'm looking forward to telling him about the band rehearsal. As I gaze around in my boredom, I wonder what else this office is used for. There are stacks of box files marked A to Z on metal shelving which means there must be twenty-six of them. Can't imagine that Q and Z get used very much. There's a musty smell in here of old paper and rubber bands and pencil shavings and, everything looks like it could do with a good clean.

'Hi!' Adam crashes into the office pulling me from my musing. He seems out of breath, as if he's been running and he smells of fresh air, as if he's been outside. He usually smells of aftershave; I don't know what it is but it's sort of musky and makes me feel a bit light headed when he's close to me.

'Hi.' I can't help beaming at him.

He closes the door with a clang and comes round and flings himself down into the chair opposite me, his long legs taking up half of the room.

'Sorry I'm late.' He gives me that lovely smile. 'Had a bit of a crisis with a client, but it's all okay now.'

I feel a stab of resentment at the thought of another client, or is it jealousy? I don't like it when he mentions other clients; he never tells me anything about them but I suppose I don't like to think of him talking to other people like he talks to me. Although I'm sure it's not the same when he's with other clients, they won't talk like we talk.

'You okay? Want a drink or anything?'

'No. I'm good, thanks.' I don't think I'd want a drink out of the rusty old kettle sitting on top of the filing cabinet and who knows where we'd get water from.

See how easily we talk to each other now? We get on so well, as if we've known each other forever.

'So,' he says, interlocking his fingers and stretching his arms above his head, 'How is the band doing?'

I've been keeping Adam up to date on the rehearsals; just over a week to go now until gig night. I'm sort of looking forward to it because I think Tourists of Reality are good and they deserve to play in front of an audience and get some applause. At my last session I nearly asked Adam if he'd come and watch them but I stopped myself just in time. As if someone like him would want to come and watch a college band. But then I think, I don't know, maybe he *would* want to come because he is a sort of friend really, isn't he?

'Rehearsals are going well and I'm not feeling so anxious about it all. I'm *almost* looking forward to it.'

'That's great! They're so lucky to have you as a manager – the Old Vic was the place to go when I was a student. All the up and coming bands played there.'

I was totally honest and told Adam that Dad got them the gig, not me. But Adam said the way he sees it everyone needs a bit of help when they first take on a job and there's nothing wrong with a helping hand. He says it's just a matter of confidence, that as my confidence grows, I'll be able to go out and talk to people, get the band gigs by myself.

'Yeah, only a week to go. You should come and watch them.' As soon as I've said it, I could just kill myself. Adam won't meet my eyes and looks uncertain. Idiot. Of course he doesn't want to come, why would he?

'Yeah, sure, sounds like a plan.' He says it casually but still won't meet my eyes. I could just die. Why did I say it?

Still avoiding looking at me he rummages around in his backpack on the floor and pulls his notebook and pen out. He sits back up and flips it open and studies the page. He obviously can't even look at me and I can feel my face starting to burn.

After what feels like forever, he finally looks up with a smile on his face. 'Exams? Last time we didn't have time to talk about your exams.'

I've been dreading talking about this but now I feel like he's thrown me a lifeline. We can forget that I stupidly asked him to a gig. A horrific though occurs to me - did he think I'd asked him like, on a date? OMG kill me now. My face feels even hotter.

'Josie?' He's looking at me with concern. 'Do you think you can do that? Tell me what happened with your exams?'

'Yes.' I swallow, might as well get it over with. 'Basically, everyone thinks I failed them on purpose.'

Adam nods. It's hardly a surprise.

'Did you?'

No! But I know that no-one believes me, not even Dad. Probably because I haven't told anyone what really happened. I still can't understand it even now. I was a shoo-in to get all A stars. I'm not bragging, just stating a fact. I've been blessed with a near photographic memory so it's not like I even have to swot up on stuff, I just remember it. Not instantly; sometimes it takes a little while, but it's all there, just waiting to be selected and used.

'No.'

I'd like to say it was deliberate, that I was making

some grand gesture because that's what everyone thinks; that I did it on purpose. But I didn't.

'You left every page blank, never wrote anything at all?'

It's true. I remember the first exam, it was English Literature. I sat down, they started the clock and I turned the paper over and started to read. I must have read that paper twenty times but I couldn't make sense of it, the words tumbled around the page and just wouldn't stay still so I could read them. I can still feel the rising panic that I felt then, frantically trying to read the questions and not having a clue what I was supposed to do. When the invigilator told us to put down our pens, I realised that I hadn't even picked mine up.

I turned the paper face down on the desk and walked out with everyone else but I felt I was someone else, somewhere else. The next exam was the same, they were all the same. I tell this to Adam, he listens without comment until I've finished.

'Okay.' He taps his lips with his index finger.

'Are you afraid it'll happen again?'

I nod dumbly, unable to speak. I'm so frightened it'll happen again and I'll never be able to pass anything. Ever.

'Have you ever had a panic attack?'

I shake my head.

'I think what you've described is a kind of panic attack.'

'No.' I shake my head emphatically. 'I don't think so. I've seen panic attacks, a girl at school used to have them, she had to blow into a paper bag to calm herself down.'

Adams smiles. 'There are different types of panic

attacks, you couldn't think straight, you panicked.'

'But I was calm to start with. It was only when I couldn't read the questions that I felt any panic.'

'Why couldn't you read the questions?

'I don't know.'

'I do. Because you panicked, you couldn't think straight and panicked some more. Classic panic circle.'

Sort of makes sense. But it'll happen again, I know it will.

'You think it'll happen again.' He reads my mind.

'There are coping strategies, things I could teach you that'll help.'

I almost believe him. I want to believe him.

'Honestly, you don't need to worry. You're in a much better place now than you were a year ago, you've moved on. Look at you, you've improved so much in the last few weeks.'

It's true, I am much better than I was; I'm getting better. Maybe it doesn't have to happen again, maybe he can help.

'Next session I'll bring some information on coping strategies, we'll go through them together, make sure you've got the coping mechanisms to ensure it doesn't happen again.

'Thanks.' I manage a small smile.

'Just remember you're not alone Josie, I'm here for you.'

We'll go through them together, he said, he's there for me. But he doesn't say that to his other clients.

I wake up and it's pitch black; I have no idea what time it is and for some unexplained reason I feel suddenly afraid. I reach my hand out and grope around for the switch and put the bedside lamp on and the familiar contours of my room emerge from the gloom. The sound of Skipper snoring gently at the end of the bed reassures me and I reach down and rub his fur and he snuffles and then resumes snoring. I can just make out the faint pattern of one of my socks clamped underneath his paws. I look at the numbers on the alarm clock, 3:27.

I'm not sure what woke me, it may have been a dream but whatever it was it's gone now, vanished into the night. After Mum died, I used to wake like this a lot, but then it was always nightmares that used to wake me. Nightmares of Mum and trains, the whoosh of a train hurtling towards me and horrible visions of Mum jumping onto the tracks and screaming that it was the only way she could be free of us. Jumbled thoughts of grief made into nightmares.

I've been sleeping a lot better lately and yesterday was a good day. After my counselling with Adam I went back to my classes and then watched the band rehearse again. I can't see why I would wake up like this when I had such a good day.

That's a lie, I do know why. Yesterday's counselling was a breakthrough, I'd never told anyone about what happened in the exams, but after I'd told Adam I felt like a weight had been lifted; I felt so much better. I think I may even be able to talk to Dad about it.

And that's why I've woken up; because there's this voice in my head that keeps saying; if you feel so much better after talking about what happened in the exams why don't you tell Adam about Mum? Maybe it would help.

But I can't. It would be so disloyal and I don't want him to judge her. He never knew Mum and he'd have a perception of her that isn't anything like she really was.

I wish I didn't know. If only I hadn't answered the phone, then I would never have suspected. The phone was quietly put down and even then, I wouldn't have guessed if Mum hadn't given herself away. The silent phone calls happened a few times, nothing so strange in that is there? I saw the worried look on Mum's face when it happened but even then I wouldn't have known for sure if it wasn't for the card. If it hadn't been for the birthday card, I might never have put two and two together.

Mum's birthday fell on a Saturday, we were getting ready to go out for lunch at her favourite pasta restaurant. We'd had such a lovely morning, Dad had cooked us salmon and scrambled egg for breakfast, making his usual mess in the kitchen, and then we'd sat on the sofa while Mum unwrapped her presents from us. Dad had bought her a beautiful blue cashmere jumper and I gave her a blue beaded bracelet to go with it. I remember her laughing when she opened her present of socks from Skipper and said what a good job he'd done of the wrapping up with his paws. But I also remember that she got a bit tearful, said how lucky she was to have such a fantastic family. Looking back, was that because she was thinking of leaving us or because she wished she was with him?

Dad went upstairs to have a shower and Mum and I were sitting chatting when the post arrived. I jumped up to go and get it because I knew there'd be loads of birthday cards for Mum and I knew she'd be looking for the one from Nanny and Grandad. They retired to Spain five years ago and I know Mum missed them like mad. We'd go and stay with them for a couple of weeks every year and we were always sad to leave. I picked the cards up from the doormat and took them into Mum and she sat and opened them, showing me each one after she'd read them. Except for one; she opened it and slid it underneath the empty envelopes. She thought I hadn't seen, but I had. I wish I hadn't. She had a strange look on her face too, she looked almost frightened. She must have been afraid of getting found out.

While she went upstairs to get ready to go out, I arranged all of her birthday cards around the room. Once I'd done that I started to wonder who the mysterious birthday card was from and what she'd done with it. So I went looking. I didn't have to look very far; Dad was upstairs so I guessed she hadn't taken it up there and she'd been out to the kitchen to take her coffee cup out so that's where I looked.

I found it quite easily; it was in the bin underneath the empty envelopes from her birthday cards. She'd torn it in half then in half again but I pieced it together on the worktop. I knew instantly and the silent phone calls suddenly made sense. The handwriting was quite large and l remember thinking it untidy, almost childish. It said:

To my darling Nessa, wishing you the best Birthday ever. I wish we could spend it together. Not long now my love.

It wasn't signed but there were lots of X's in the shape of a heart.

I felt sick and couldn't believe what I was seeing. Suddenly everything was ruined and the whole day disappeared into a big black hole and I just wanted to cry and cry.

Then I started to get angry. How dare he send it to our house where Dad and I might see it, or was that the plan, to force Mum to tell us? I couldn't believe how Mum had betrayed us, how she'd sat and opened her presents and said how lucky she was to have us. All lies! While she was lying to us, she was wishing she was with *him,* wishing she could spend her birthday with him.

I was still standing there when I heard Dad coming down the stairs, whistling an unrecognisable tune. I quickly picked up the pieces of card and shoved them back in the bin and put the envelopes on top. I composed myself and never said anything but the rest of the day was torture. Mum knew something was wrong and kept asking me if I was okay; I told her I didn't feel very well but really, I wanted to shout at her and tell her I knew. But I couldn't.

For the rest of the weekend I pretended I was ill and mostly stayed in my room. Sunday lasted forever and as I stayed in my room with the door shut, I wondered what the hell I was going to do, wondered if Mum was going to leave us. Half of me felt guilty for ruining Mum's birthday and the other half of me hated her, hated her for what she'd done.

And then I didn't have to wonder anymore; on the Monday Mum was dead and I never got the chance to talk to her again.

Chapter 9

Josie

Louise is taking me with her to her hairdresser, Dolph. We were chatting this morning while doing the archiving and she was saying she was getting her hair cut this afternoon and I just mentioned how I needed a trim. I was just making conversation really but now she's insisting that I go with her and get mine done too and she's assured me that Dolph won't mind and will fit me in. She says she's texted him and he doesn't mind at all, but I'm wishing now that I'd kept my mouth shut.

I'm feeling awkward about just turning up – and I don't really know him and he's a *man* - but I can't really get out of it now. I'm also not sure why I'm even bothering because I always tie it back in a ponytail anyway and could probably just snip the split ends off myself.

We're going to her house first to drop Sprocket off then over to the outskirts of town where Dolph has his salon. I'm sitting in the front passenger seat with Sprocket on my lap. He was on the back seat but once we'd got going, he jumped into the front and onto me and started licking my face. Louise was going to pull over and put him in the back but I said I didn't mind, he's no problem, although I don't really want my face licked so I'm stroking him and that seems to calm him down.

We pull up outside Louise's house and she yanks the handbrake on and leaves the engine ticking over. 'Won't be a minute, I'll just chuck him in and I'll be straight back.'

She opens the car door and beckons Sprocket but he doesn't move and he lies down on me like a dead weight with his paws dangling over the seat.

'Come *on*.'

Sprocket still doesn't move and Louise has to resort to coming round to the passenger door and dragging him out of the car by his collar. He looks at me with his big brown eyes and I have to look away. Poor Sprocket, he clearly doesn't want to go.

I watch out of the window as Louise drags him up the path and opens the front door and oofs him inside. Within a few minutes she's back and as she gets in the car, I can hear the faint sound of Sprocket howling.

'Bloody dog.' Louise puts the car into gear. 'Can't bear to be on his own for five minutes. Worse than a kid.'

We rattle off down the road.

'My friend Biro lives round here. Do you know The George? His Dad runs it.'

'Oh yeah, it's a couple of streets away, been there a few times. I think I've seen your mate – very tall with curly hair and wears a fur coat?'

'Yeah that's Biro, you can't really miss him.'

Louise laughs. 'He does stand out a bit.'

We suddenly swerve into a narrow lane and zoom along it missing the bushes by inches on each side. Seems like a weird place to have a hairdressing salon.

We come out of the lane onto an even narrower lane where a row of terraced cottages overlooks a small field. We pull up in front of the end cottage and after much toing and froing Louise parks the car a foot from the kerb.

'I hate parallel parking. Nightmare. Right, here we are.' Louise pulls the handbrake on and reaches over and grabs her handbag from the back seat.

'Okay?'

'Er, yeah.' I open the door and get out of the car.

'Not what you were expecting?'

'No, not really.'

'Dolph works from home,' Louise says as we walk up to the front door. 'And he's very selective about whose hair he cuts.' She rings the bell.

So he probably won't want to cut mine then. I'm beginning to wish I hadn't come.

The door is eventually opened very slowly by a middle-aged man in a brown cardigan, rust coloured corduroy trousers and a brown and yellow striped tie. He looks like a not very happy schoolteacher, not a hairdresser.

'Hello! Come in, come in. And who is your young friend, Louise?' He breaks into a smile and it completely transforms him and I realise he's not as old as I thought.

'Hello, Bertie, how are you? This is Josie, my friend from work. Josie, meet Bertie.' Bertie kisses her on both cheeks. I desperately hope that he's not going to kiss me.

'Hi, Bertie.' So he's not the hairdresser.

'Hello darling, nice to meet you.' He presses my hand and thankfully makes no move to kiss me.

Once inside the three of us stand in the tiny hallway

that's so small we're practically nose to nose. I try not to get anxious about having no personal space and tell myself that it won't be for long. There are peach carpeted stairs directly in front of us with a door on either side. The door to the right is suddenly pulled open and a very tall man wearing a powder blue tracksuit appears and grabs Louise by the hand and pulls her through the doorway.

'Darling! Come through! I hope Bertie's not boring you to death. Is this the lovely Josie? Come!' He swivels on one foot and we follow him as he strides across a vast kitchen to a door at the other end of the room. The kitchen has a space age feel, all glossy white cupboards and stainless steel. Dolph flings his arm up theatrically like a ballet dancer as he calls back over his shoulder. 'We'll have tea in exactly an hour, Bertie.' He doesn't even turn around.

I have to nearly run to keep up with his giant strides and follow him and Louise into a square room. It's a mini hair salon, one sink to wash hair with one chair facing a wall mirror. Completely different from the kitchen, no state-of-the-art stainless steel here. Blood-red painted walls and brightly coloured throws and cushions are piled on an old fashioned over stuffed sofa wedged into one corner. A huge pile of magazines rest on a small table next to the sofa and a radio is playing the same channel that Dad listens to. You know, the one for old people. A very large tabby cat is curled up on one half of the sofa.

'Right, darlings. Louise, I'll do you first. Josie, chuck the cat on the floor and have a pew.' I try to move the cat but it won't budge so I sort of squash up next to it. I think it's asleep. Or dead.

'So, Louise, what's it to be?'

He pulls Louise's hair up by the ends, and fluffs the top up a bit then lets it drop.

'Just the usual, Dolph, not too much off.'

'You sure? Can't tempt you with something different?'

Louise shakes her head. I pick up a magazine and flick through it while Dolph starts snipping away at Louise's hair. He talks constantly and I listen in and discover that Bertie is his partner and that they have three cats, Bertie *is* a schoolteacher, just as I thought. Dolph would love to have a dog just like Sprocket but Bertie's not sure because he doesn't think the cats will like it.

It's nice and warm in this little room and when the drone of the hairdryer starts, I find my eyelids growing heavy. I could easily drift off to sleep; the result of waking up at 3:30 this morning.

Dolph has just finished Louise's hair when Bertie brings a tray of tea in. We sit and drink it out of rose patterned cups and saucers and eat biscuits which Dolph tells me are garibaldi, his favourite.

'Your hair looks lovely, Louise.' It does too.

'Ta. Dolph's the only one who can manage to make my hair halfway decent which is why I come out here to the sticks.'

Dolph looks mock shocked. 'Halfway decent? I'm insulted! I don't work my magic on just anyone, you know.' He arches an eyebrow and winks at me.

'Now…' He drains his cup and puts it down. 'Time to swap seats. Over here sweets and let's have a look at you.'

I take Louise's seat and she shoves the cat off the sofa and settles herself down. It was alive then.

Dolph pulls the elastic band out and ruffles his hand

through my hair then pulls it around my face so it touches my shoulders.

'So what do you want doing, darling?' He tugs my hair down at the back.

'Just a trim, I say. 'I usually just put it up in a ponytail.'

He purses his lips and blows out through his nose like a horse.

'Hmm. Is this your natural colour? It's not coloured is it?'

'No.'

'Thought not. It's in lovely condition, natural highlights, sort of strawberry blonde.' He stands back and studies me. He frowns, then studies me some more and I start to feel a bit uncomfortable.

'You have a look of a blonde Audrey Hepburn about you.'

'Who?'

He tuts. 'Sacrilege. Can you hear this Louise? She's never heard of Audrey Hepburn.'

Louise laughs, 'Not surprised Dolph, she was before my time and yours, never mind Josies.'

'So who was she?' I ask.

'Only one of the most beautiful women in the world.'

I watch in the mirror as he pulls my hair up and back, then lets it drop and purses his lips again and frowns.

'Okay. I'm afraid I'm not going to be able to trim your hair. Not possible.'

He stands behind me and I watch in the mirror as he folds his arms.

'Oh.' I don't know what to say. Are his scissors broken or something? OMG, I haven't got nits, have I?

I know there was a rumour going around college that one of the Taylor twins had them. I feel my face start to burn.

'No. I can cut it for you, but not trim it.'

Thank God, not nits. 'What does that mean?' I say and I can see Louise in the mirror watching us carefully from the armchair.

'Are you feeling brave? And adventurous? Because if you are, I will cut your hair and you will look fabulous, you will see all of the lovely natural highlights. But I will not *trim* it so you can scuff it up in a ponytail. So…the question is; are you brave enough?'

I'm not brave. Or adventurous. It's taken all of my courage to take my Parka off and I didn't even want my hair trimmed, if I'm being honest.

'Okay,' I say, 'Do whatever you like to it.'

We're in Louise's car on the way home and it's very quiet.

I have no hair left. Dolph snipped and cut, snipped and cut and now my hair is so short I look like a boy.

So much for being brave. I will be wearing my Parka with the hood up until it grows again. So probably for the next two years.

'You okay? Josie?' Louise looks at me with concern.

I nod, not trusting myself to speak in case I burst into tears.

'Don't you like your hair?'

I shake my head. My ponytail used to swish when I did that.

'It looks lovely, Josie. Amazing. It's just a shock when you first see it, you'll be used to it by tomorrow. Even the colour looks different. You should put your hood down, show it off.'

At least I didn't have to pay, Dolph wouldn't let me, said he'd enjoyed creating a new me and wouldn't dream of charging me, said he enjoyed doing it.

More like it's so awful he didn't feel he could make me pay for it.

We pull up outside my house.

'Thanks for the lift, and for taking me.' I try to sound like I mean it because it was nice of Louise but how I wish I hadn't gone and I still had some hair left.

'My pleasure, hun. See you next Saturday.'

I get out of the car and stand and wave as the car disappears down the street.

I quietly let myself into the house to see Dad in the kitchen getting our tea ready. He's doing his usual thing of chopping onions with a pair of swimming goggles on so they don't make him cry.

'Hello sweetheart, did you have a nice time? I'm doing a chilli.' He calls over his shoulder. He sounds like he's got a peg on his nose. Skipper trots over to me and I bend down and rub his ears then pick him up and bury my face in his fur. His wagging tail thumps on my arm as I hold him.

'Fine.' I put Skipper down and straighten up and undo my coat and take it off. Might as well get it over with.

I stand there and wait.

After forever Dad finally turns around and looks at me. He opens his mouth to speak and then just stares at me; his mouth hanging open. He slowly takes his goggles off and stares some more.

'Oh my God.' He says.

See, told you it was bad.

I was looking forward to tonight's rehearsal but now I

just need to get through it and get home. I rummaged around in Dad's wardrobe and finally found a black beanie hat which I'm wearing as well as keeping the hood up. I've pulled the front of the hat down to just above my eyebrows.

After Dad got over the shock, he tried to say it was lovely but he's not fooling me, the look of horror on his face said it all. In the safety of the bathroom I tried to do something with it but it's so short I could do *nothing*. It was hardly worth trying to comb it, it's so short. It'll take forever to grow and all of my good intentions about not wearing my Parka all the time have gone. I'll have to wear it in the summer as well or maybe get a thinner one with a hood or else I might melt.

I'm absolutely dreading going to college on Monday; the Clackers will keep on and on about it and once they see how it upsets me, they won't let it go. I feel sick when I imagine Shana's reaction to my hair.

When I arrive for the rehearsal, I can tell Biro isn't fooled one bit by the beanie hat. I'm the last to arrive because I've mucked around in the bathroom for so long trying to make it look less short.

'What's with the hat?' Biro looks at me suspiciously.

'Got earache.'

'Should you be here listening to us? With earache?'

'Can't miss it, can I?' I say while sitting down out of his eyeline. 'Can't have a full-on rehearsal without the manager.'

Biro just shrugs.

Danny gives me a hesitant smile but doesn't say anything about the hat and Mogs, well, Mogs wouldn't notice if a bomb dropped on him as long as it didn't damage his guitar.

I sit and watch as they run through their set, they're playing so well together and it's amazing how much they've improved. Danny looks so convincing pretending to play his guitar. It's getting warm in here and my head's starting to itch so I stick one finger inside the hat and have a good scratch.

'Bit hot?' I nearly jump out of my skin, Biro is standing in front of me.

'No. I'm fine.'

He slides down the wall and sits down next to me.

'Mate, I'm used to your weirdness and everything but take the hat off.'

'No.'

'Why not?'

'Because I've had my hair cut and I look like a boy.'

'Take it off.'

'No.'

'At least put your hood down.'

I reluctantly pull the hood down. At least it's not so hot. It suddenly feels even cooler when Biro whips the hat off my head and jumps up, holding the hat out of my reach.

'Biro!' I scream at him. 'Give me it back!'

'Well,' says Biro thoughtfully, staring at me.

Danny and Mogs look at Biro to see what the fuss is about and then follow Biro's eyes to me.

'I will never forgive you for this Biro, you're supposed to be my friend.' I can feel myself starting to blush.

'You had your hair cut or something Josie?' Mogs stares at me, blinking through his curtains of hair. 'Something different about you but I can't put my finger on it.'

'She's had it all chopped off, dude. She looks like a

little pixie.' Biro laughs. 'But it suits you, sort of cute.'

'Oh, yeah,' says Mogs looking at me intently. 'I can see it now.'

Danny steps in front of Biro and Mogs and stares down at me.

I wait silently, bring it on, get it all over with.

'I think she looks beautiful,' he says.

Chapter 10

Robbie

I thought I'd seen a ghost.

I always wear swimming goggles for chopping onions because they make my eyes run something terrible. I don't actually wear them for swimming – I think they look naff to be honest. Anyway, I was feeling a lot better than I had for a long time; not exactly happy, but sort of on the way to being happy. Josie seems to have turned a corner and come out of herself a bit and I suppose I was feeling a little bit optimistic about things getting better, getting back to something like normal. A new normal.

I heard the front door open so I knew it was Josie and I called out a hello to her but when I turned round and saw her; my God, for a moment I thought it *was* Nessa, what with the goggles being a bit misty. For a split second I thought she'd come back to me.

Yes, I know. Bloody stupid.

Of course as soon as I took the goggles off, I could see that it was Josie, and of course I knew it wasn't Nessa really, it couldn't possibly be Nessa. The sensible part of me knew that it wasn't her but just for a moment she looked so like my Nessa. And in that split second, I felt everything; elation that she'd come back and horror that she was never coming back.

Josie's little heart shaped face with those enormous blue eyes and that haircut - Nessa had really short hair when we first met and I used to make her laugh when I called her my little pixie.

Josie wouldn't believe me when I said her hair looked lovely. She thought I was looking at her in horror and I didn't want to tell her the real reason because that would have upset her even more so all in all I made a right mess of everything. Now she thinks she looks awful and that everyone's going to laugh at her and make fun of her. And that little bit of confidence that she's worked so hard to get in the last few weeks has gone and it's my fault.

At least she *went* to the rehearsal; that's the thing with our Josie, she takes her responsibilities seriously. If she wasn't band manager there's no way she'd have gone. When I dropped her off for the band rehearsal, she was wearing one of my old beanie hats and that bloody Parka. I could kick myself, I really could. I'm such an idiot. I said to her, you can't wear that hat forever you know; your hair will take months to grow.

And she just gave me that *look*, and I thought; she will, she'll be wearing that hat for the next six months.

One step forward and two steps back.

Chapter 11

Josie

I could hear them at the back of the room, sniggering and whispering. I swear I could even smell Shana's fruity bubble gum although I knew it wasn't really possible.

I couldn't concentrate on anything this morning because I knew that Shana and Stacey were sitting behind me at the back of the class laughing at my hair. As soon as the tutorial ended, I hurried out of the classroom and made my way straight to the canteen.

I'm sitting with Biro at our usual table but I know that it's only a brief respite; I've no doubt that Shana and Stacey will make it their mission to come and find me.

I intended wearing the beanie hat to college but I think that would have been more noticeable than the hair and I can hardly wear it for the next six months, can I? I'd look pretty ridiculous wearing a hat in the summer. Also, it itched like mad. So. No hat, no hood, let them all have a good look and get the laughing and looks over with.

And I've definitely had some looks, even some gob dropping double takes, and when I look around, I can see why. All the other girls have either long hair or swishy bob type hairstyles, not short back and earholes, not boy cuts, like me.

I suppose I have to thank Biro, really. If he hadn't whipped my hat off on Saturday, I don't think I would have been brave enough to leave the house hatless and front it out. After Danny's comment at the rehearsal we were all speechless. Danny surprised me even more, his face was beetroot but he didn't try to take back what he'd said; just shrugged and said that it was his opinion, and left it at that. It was a bit awkward for a little while but once they started playing again things soon got back to normal. But I keep remembering what he said and the way he said it. No one has ever said I was beautiful (apart from Mum and Dad and obviously they don't count). More to the point no boy has ever said that about me or paid me a compliment. I've decided that I'm not going to obsess over it and ruin things like I usually do; I'm just going to enjoy it.

'Mind if we join you?' The Clackers have arrived; Shana, Stacey and Ellie hover at the end of the table holding their trays.

Biro ignores them and carries on eating so I attempt a careless shrug and give a weak smile.

Shana slides into the seat next to me and Stacey sits next to Biro. Ellie dumps her tray onto the table with a bang and trudges off to get a chair.

'You look different.' Shana puts her head on one side and stares at me with a puzzled look. 'Have you had your hair cut Josie?' She raises one of her expertly pencilled-in eyebrows.

Bitch.

'No.' I deadpan. Don't know where that came from, didn't mean to say that at all.

Shana frowns although I hear a quickly stifled snigger from Ellie as she reappears with a chair.

Shana stabs a lettuce leaf with her fork and twirls it around and inspects it.

'It's a bit drastic isn't it? Bit short. Like a boy. I bet you can't wait for it to grow.'

Stacey gives an insipid giggle which spurs Shana on.

'I mean, you wouldn't want to be mistaken for a boy, would you?' She takes a delicate bite from the lettuce leaf with her perfect teeth.

'Actually,' I say, 'I love it.'

Shana looks at me in shock.

'I think it looks great, Josie,' Ellie chips in. 'It really suits you.'

I can't help smiling. I feel ridiculously pleased that Ellie's stuck up for me.

Shana gives Ellie a look of pure venom.

'Yea, looks sort of cool,' says Stacey.

'Bit boyish though,' she adds hurriedly when she sees Shana glaring at her.

And I'm thinking; I've done it, I've done the first day with my short hair and the worst is over. I feel my stomach untie from the knots it's tangled itself in and realise that I might actually be able to eat something.

'Are you eating *all* of that Ellie?' Shana points at Ellie's plate of shepherd's pie. 'Only it's really fattening.'

'Er, probably.' Ellie gives Shana a puzzled look.

'Yeah, thought so.' Shana bursts out laughing and looks meaningfully at Stacey who joins in the laughter.

Ellie blushes bright red. I knew Shana would make her pay for taking my side.

'Well if you ask me,' Biro's booming voice cuts across Shana and Stacey's giggling. 'You could do with a bit of shepherd's pie yourself instead of that rabbit food.'

Shana puts down the partly nibbled lettuce leaf on her plate. 'Oh, I couldn't. I have to watch what I eat, *I* don't want to get fat.' She looks pointedly at Ellie when she says *fat*.

'Ellie's not fat at all, but you're a bitch.'

Shana stares at Biro opened mouthed, unable to believe what she's hearing.

'I'm not a ...' she starts to say.

'And in future,' Biro goes on loudly, 'Go and sit somewhere else if all you can do is slag people off.'

I'm sitting in the counselling room waiting for Adam to arrive. I'm not early this time, he's late. I know the way now but it still seems a long trek from the main part of the college.

I've taken my coat off; how brave of me! I'm wearing a deep blue fluffy jumper that Auntie Bridget bought me for Christmas. It's long and loose and feels so comfortable and I don't know why I haven't worn it before. I've pretty much worn the same few boring sweatshirts for the past year but last night I thought, right, the hair is gone maybe the sweatshirts should go too.

Time to *make an effort* as Mum used to say. I went through my wardrobe and got all of the new stuff out that I've never worn and tried it all on. And I have to agree with Dad – what you wear can help you to feel better about yourself. I tried this jumper on and looked in the mirror and I though, actually, you don't look too bad, even the hair looked a bit less awful.

I wonder what Adam will think of it? I wonder if he'll think I look beautiful like Danny? Which is a stupid thing to think, because of course he won't, I don't know why I even thought that.

I hear Adam's heavy footsteps coming down the corridor and the door behind me opens and I turn around to see Adam coming in. His smile freezes when he sees me and my own greeting dies on my lips.

He sits down opposite me and crosses his legs in his usual manner and stares at me.

'You hate it don't you?'

He shakes his head.

'It's too short.'

'No. It's not. It's just a shock.'

I *knew* he'd hate it. I choke down bitter disappointment; I so desperately wanted him to like it. I should have kept my coat on, I could have put the hood up and then he'd never have seen my awful hair. And why did I even wear this stupid jumper? Was I actually trying to *impress* him?

'You look so different.'

'Like a boy,' I say miserably.

Adam laughs, a low throaty laugh.

'No. *Definitely* not like a boy.'

'You don't hate it then?' I ask hopefully.

'Hate it? Of course not. It suits you.'

It's a relief he doesn't hate it but I can't help feeling disappointed. Was I expecting him to compliment me like Danny did? I feel awkward and uncomfortable and I don't quite know what to do. I focus my eyes on the out of date calendar on the wall while Adam opens his notebook and rifles through the pages. Finally, he speaks.

'How have you been coping since last week?'

'Okay, I think I am slowly improving.'

He nods thoughtfully and scribbles in his notebook. I try to see what he writes but he has it tipped away from me.

He looks up. 'So, what prompted the hair cut? Or had you been planning it for a while?'

It's the sort of thing he asks each session but there's something different, something I can't put my finger on. Am I imagining it? No, I'm not. I have the feeling that Adam's annoyed with me, that I've done something wrong but I have no idea what it is.

'No, it was a spur of the moment thing. I was only supposed to be having a trim but got talked into something more drastic.'

I tell him about Dolph, and Bertie and Louise. Then I tell him about the beanie hat and he laughs at that and things seem to get back to normal.

'I'd decided to wear the beanie hat until my hair grew again.'

'Might have been a bit difficult in the summer.'

'I know!'

'What made you change your mind?'

I tell him about the rehearsal and how Biro pulled the hat off me.

'How did that make you feel?'

'I was fuming,' I say. 'But I think he did me a favour really.'

'He did,' Adam agrees. 'But I think you would have done it anyway in your own time because your confidence is growing.'

And because a part of me wants to show off, I tell him about what Danny said. Maybe I just want Adam to know that someone paid me a compliment. I don't know, but the minute I've said it I wish I hadn't because it makes me sound like a vain idiot.

'It's a nice compliment, but remember, you don't need anyone else's approval for your appearance.'

'I know that.' I wish I hadn't told him now.

'You don't need a spotty teenager to boost your low self-esteem.' Adam's looking very serious. 'You have your own self-worth.'

Danny's not spotty at all and I just think he was being nice but now I feel deflated. Is my self-esteem so low that only other people can make me feel better?

'Why do you think Danny paid you the compliment?'

I shrug. 'Danny's really nice, he was just being nice.'

'Guys don't generally pay compliments just to be nice.'

'What do you mean?'

'He's obviously attracted to you, are you attracted to him?'

'No! He's just a friend.'

'Might be best if you let him know that, in case he gets the wrong idea.'

Now I'm going to feel awkward around Danny because Adam's said that; I hadn't even thought of Danny in that way.

'He doesn't fancy me, he can have his pick of girls, he's really hot.'

Adam doesn't look at me and continues scribbling in the notebook. The silence grows and stretches and I start to feel more and more uncomfortable. I wish I could start the session again and not mention Danny or the stupid compliment.

Adam looks up at last. 'So now we have to talk about the elephant in the room.'

'What?'

'The elephant in the room that we never talk about. Your mother.'

'Oh.'

'You're not going to progress unless you can be completely honest with me about your feelings for her.'

'I have been honest.'

'How would you describe your relationship with your mother?'

'Very close. We were very close.'

'You could tell each other anything?'

'Oh yes, I could confide in Mum about anything. She always made me feel better if something was troubling me. I could always talk to Dad as well but me and Mum were even closer.'

'Good, good. And was it mutual? Did she confide in you about things that were troubling her?'

I hesitate for just for a second but it's long enough for Adam to notice.

'Josie, you do know you can tell me anything? Whatever you tell me is completely confidential and will never leave this room.'

'I know.' I wish I had my coat on. I'd pull the hood up now.

Adam leans forward in his chair and stares at me so intently that I can't look away.

'So, tell me what it is that's really bothering you.'

Chapter 12

Josie

Friday's come around so quickly; too quickly. I'm on the way to my session with Adam and for the first time ever I don't want to go. Part of me wants to see him but something has changed, but I don't know what.

I saw Adam in the canteen yesterday; Biro and I were sitting at our usual table when I happened to look up and I saw Adam across the room. He was standing in front of the doors talking to one of the tutors and although they were deep in conversation, I know that he must have seen me because I wasn't that far away from him. I'm sure he looked right at me. I put my hand up in a wave and he totally blanked me, looked straight through me as if I wasn't there. I felt proper stupid and turned the wave into brushing my hand over my head as if I was smoothing my non-existent hair.

'I know him,' Biro had said following my gaze.

'What?'

'That guy you're staring at, I know him. He used to live in our street, a couple of doors down from us.'

'Did he?'

'Yeah. I think he's a bit old for you though.'

I gave a fake laugh. 'Don't be stupid, I don't fancy

him.'

'You want to tell your face that,' Biro had said seriously.

'I was just waving to him but I don't think he saw me.' I lower my voice. 'He's my counsellor.'

'Is he?' Biro had looked over at Adam in surprise. 'I never knew he was a counsellor, he doesn't look the type. Whatever's he's doing it seems to be working. Just remember he's a counsellor and not your friend. It's his job.'

'I know that, I'm not stupid,' I said, and then I started gabbling because I was on the defensive. 'I think it's definitely helping. Probably because he knows how I feel; he lost his mum when he was about the same age as me.' I'd felt I needed to justify myself; the comment that I fancied him was making me feel uncomfortable. I should have just shut up because I can't get anything past Biro.

Biro picked up his drink and took a slurp while giving me a level look.

'His mum and dad still live a couple of doors away.' He took another slurp of his drink. 'Though that'd be his stepmum I suppose'.

'Yeah, I don't think his dad wasted any time in finding someone else.' I'd immediately felt guilty for saying it, Adam had told me that in confidence and I've just blabbed it to Biro without a moment's thought. I must learn to either keep my mouth shut or say it and not feel guilty.

I'd changed the subject and started talking about the band then so that I could get Biro off the subject of Adam but I could tell that he wasn't fooled. I'm rubbish at lying. Will I be able to lie convincingly today? I know that Adam will want me to talk about Mum but I don't want to. I'd manage to talk about Mum at the last session without actually telling him anything but I think Adam knows that I'm holding back and I don't know how much longer I *can* hold back.

I do feel so much better but talking about Mum is not going to help because if I tell the truth about her, I'm going to feel so disloyal. Adam will judge her and I won't be able to bear it. He might say he won't judge her but the truth is he won't be able to stop himself. I want to be honest with him but I know the longer I talk about her then the more chance there is that the floodgates will open and it'll all come out.

This week should have been a good week. Once I'd got used to it, I felt brave and daring with my new hairstyle for a brief while but now I just feel shallow and pathetic for letting other people's opinions influence the way I feel. Adam is right, I should have more self-worth. The gig is tomorrow night and the way I'm going that's going to be ruined, which will be my own fault for trying to show off to Adam. If I hadn't told him about Danny then I wouldn't be feeling awkward around him in rehearsals. Adam's words keep coming back to me and now I can't even look at Danny without blushing. It's obviously catching because now we hardly even talk and we got on really well before.

I slow my steps as I get nearer the counselling room; instead of wishing it wasn't so out of the way and such a long way to walk I wish it was even further away so it would take even longer to get there. I stand outside the door for a moment, take a deep breath and walk into the room. I'm surprised to see Adam is already there, sitting in his chair, waiting for me.

'Hello,' I say with a smile that I don't feel, closing the door.

'Hi.'

I sling my coat onto the back of the chair and sit down.

'So how are things going?'

'Good.' Apart from you blanking me in the canteen. I feel suddenly angry, I expect that sort of treatment from the Clackers, not Adam. I know he saw me.

Adam nods thoughtfully.

'Any more compliments about your hair?'

Isn't this a strange question to start a counselling session with? I think he's mocking me?

'Why did you ignore me in the canteen?' I blurt out, surprising myself with the anger in my voice. 'You saw me and ignored me even though I waved at you.' There, I've said it now, it's out in the open.

Adam is quiet for a moment.

'I'm sorry,' he says quietly. 'I wasn't ignoring you, it was a difficult situation.'

Oh. I'd expected him to deny seeing me or even to laugh at me. Thinking back, he *was* having a very intense conversation, almost an argument. I've seen the tutor around but I don't have any classes with her. She teaches hair and beauty, or something like that, she's quite young and really pretty with perfect hair and a perfect figure. With a stab of jealousy, it all makes sense; of course that's why he ignored me, she's probably his girlfriend and he wouldn't want to be bothered by a *client*. Why am I so surprised he has a girlfriend? Did I really think someone as good looking as him wouldn't have a girlfriend or be married?

'I'm sorry,' I say in what I hope is a grown-up way. 'Forget I said anything. I've no right to expect your time outside of counselling.'

'I'll be honest with you Josie, I was trying to

extricate myself from a difficult situation. We'd er… been out on a few dates but it was just a casual thing for me and I didn't really want to see her again. I tried to let her down gently but as you could see she wasn't very happy about it. She was demanding to know what the problem was. It was all very embarrassing.'

A bubble of happiness surges through me, so she's not his girlfriend. A part of me is telling me that this feeling of happiness is not right, Adam is my counsellor and nothing more.

'I was having difficulty calming her down and I thought she was going to start shouting at me,' he goes on. 'My counselling skills clearly weren't working.'

He's right; thinking back she was more animated than him and she did seem a bit angry and agitated.

'She's a lovely person.' Adam brushed his hand through his hair. 'But you can't choose who you have feelings for, can you?'

'No, you can't,' I say.

Adam looks down at his notepad but doesn't write anything. What he says next shocks me totally.

'I think you should find a new counsellor.'

I look at him in disbelief. 'But why? I don't want another counsellor.'

'I think I've helped you all I can.' He won't look at me, won't look up from his notebook.

'No! I can't see someone else, I can't!' I'm trying so hard not to cry, 'Is it because I said you'd ignored me? I'm sorry! I'm sorry for being so rude and childish. Please don't make me get another counsellor!'

Adam looks up from his notebook at me, his lips set in a grim line.

'I'm sorry but I can't be your counsellor anymore if you don't trust me.'

'Of course I trust you!' I almost wail at him.

'I'm sorry Josie, but you don't.'

'Why would you say that? I've told you things that I've never told anyone else.'

Adam stares at me but I can't hold his gaze and I look away.

'There, you see, you know exactly what I mean.' He folds the cover over on his notebook with an air of finality. 'If we don't have trust then there is no point.'

'I do trust you.'

'If you trust me you have to be honest with me if I'm to help you.'

He's right. I haven't told him about Mum, I skirted around the subject on Tuesday but he's not stupid, he's knows I'm avoiding something.

'If you won't counsel me then I won't have counselling anymore.'

'That's blackmail.'

'You're blackmailing me.'

'No, I'm not. I'm trying to help you. If you won't talk to me there's no point continuing with the counselling.'

I shrug. I fold my arms across my chest defensively.

'Threatening not to have counselling is also,' he looks straight at me, 'Very childish.'

I flinch under his gaze and feel myself redden.

'Sorry,' I say, 'That wasn't very fair of me. Forget I said it.'

He puts the notebook on the table and puts the pen on top then looks at his watch.

'The choice is yours, Josie.'

Betray Mum or not see Adam again?

'Okay,' I say in a shaky voice, 'I'm ready to be completely honest.'

'Good,' he says, sitting back in the chair with a smile, 'So talk to me.'

Chapter 13

Josie
'Go on, let me paint your nails.'

'No! I don't wear nail varnish.'

'Well then you should, I wouldn't leave the house without it.' Auntie Bridget holds one of her hands out in front of her and admires her plum coloured nails.

'My nails are too short and anyway, they wouldn't look like yours.'

'Course they would! These aren't real you know. Plastic. I can easily stick some on for you.'

I don't think I'd be able to pick anything up with nails that long.

'Thanks, Auntie Bridget, but I don't think they're really me.' I don't want to sound ungrateful because I know she's only trying to help.

We're at the kitchen table having just finished eating the biggest burgers ever that Dad made for tea and Uncle Ralph is noisily chomping on the half of my burger that I couldn't eat. Skipper is sitting watching with his nose about an inch from Uncle Ralph's knee.

It's the gig tonight and Auntie Bridget is trying to persuade me to let her give me a makeover.

'Leave her alone,' says Uncle Ralph through a

mouthful of burger. 'She's not a bleeding doll.'

'Stop your swearing and don't talk with your mouth full, it's disgusting.'

Uncle Ralph shrugs. 'Just saying.' He turns to Dad still chewing. 'Does that dog have to drool all over me while I'm eating?'

'Yeah, he does,' says Dad. 'Leave him some and give it to him when you've finished.'

'Na, don't believe in feeding dogs from the table.'

'You greedy sod. I can't believe how much you can pack away. You must have worms.'

Auntie Bridget watches them and rolls her eyes at me. 'Okay, if you won't have your nails done, I'll do your makeup for you.'

'Thanks, Auntie Bridget, but I don't wear makeup.'

Auntie Bridget gives a great big sigh. 'Just a touch of mascara, bit of lip gloss, a little blusher maybe?'

She's trying so hard to please me I feel mean for not letting her.

'Okay,' I say, 'Maybe just a little.'

Auntie Bridget claps her hands in delight. 'You won't regret it, you'll be the belle of the ball.'

'It's a gig night in a grotty pub not a bleeding prom.'

Auntie Bridget gives Uncle Ralph a withering look.

'Surprised they're letting you kids in anyway,' he goes on. 'You're not eighteen yet so how come you're allowed in a boozer?'

'Don't be so thick, Ralph. As long as they don't drink any alcohol they're allowed in where the bands play,' says Bridget as she turns to me. 'You're not going to drink any alcohol are you my pet?'

'Of course not,' I say. 'I don't even like the taste of it.'

Auntie Bridget smiles approvingly.

Uncle Ralph rams the last of the burger into his mouth and takes a slurp of tea.

'Banging burgers, Robbie. Got any more?'

'You're joking, aren't you?' Dad is astounded. 'I could only eat one they were so big. Where do you even put it? There's nothing of you, you're like a rake.'

'Dunno, ever since I gave up smoking I can't stop eating but I don't seem to put any weight on. Probably 'cos I'm always on the go.'

Auntie Bridget snorts. 'On the go? Don't make me laugh, you couldn't move any slower if you tried.'

'What's that supposed to mean?'

I slip away from the table unnoticed and leave them to their bickering to go upstairs to get ready. As I walk up the stairs, I can hear their voices getting louder and Dad shouting at them to pack it in.

I stand under the shower and let the water flow over me as I think back over the last couple of days.

I feel embarrassed when I remember how I told Adam that I wouldn't continue with the counselling if he wouldn't be my counsellor. He said that was blackmail; which it is. I can't believe that I said it and I instantly regretted it, I sounded like a spoilt baby. Who knew I could be so manipulative? Maybe I got it from Mum.

So I had to tell him then, about Mum, otherwise he wouldn't be my counsellor anymore and I wouldn't ever see him again. So maybe he's a bit of a blackmailer too.

Anyway, now I feel like a complete traitor to Mum and I don't feel any better at all for having got it off my chest, I feel worse. Dad doesn't even know what Mum was up to, yet I told someone who never even knew her.

Loud banging on the bathroom door interrupts my thoughts. Auntie Bridget is getting impatient.

'Josie! Are you going to be much longer?'

'No, won't be long,' I shout.

'Hurry up or we won't have time to do your makeup.'

That was the plan.

'Okay,' I shout. 'Getting out now.'

I turn the shower off and get out and towel myself dry then quickly put my underwear on. It's no good, I can't fool myself; I've let myself down trying to blackmail Adam and I feel bad for betraying Mum.

I should have just agreed to see another counsellor and kept Mum's secret. I chose Adam over Mum and I'm not feeling good about it. But it's too late now, it's done.

I grab my dressing gown from the hook on the bathroom door and wrap it around me, belting it so tight that it pinches and I have to loosen it.

No point in wallowing in guilt now, it's done. Just have to get on with it.

We go into the Vic by the back entrance and shuffle past metal chairs stacked against the wall in a narrow, shabby corridor with scuffed, peeling walls and emerge into the backstage area, which is basically a large room. There's an atmosphere of excitement and a faint smell of sweat and beer and the air is charged with nervous energy. I can hear the thump of a band playing from the bar and see flickering lights through the curtained doorway. Danny is in front of me and has the keyboard under his arms and I'm carrying the legs. Dad picked him up from his house on the way and I could tell he approved. Danny chatted politely to Dad and didn't seem bothered about all of the questions from Dad, I think he quite enjoyed talking to him. I'm trying very hard not to feel awkward around Danny; I want the easy friendship back that we had before the *compliment*.

We push our way through all of the people milling around and I can just see the top of Biro's curly topped head standing in the corner. After fighting our way through the crowd, we emerge at the back of the room to see him sitting on an upturned bucket tuning his guitar.

'Hi!'

'Yo.' He beams from ear to ear. 'Can't believe it's here, not long now.'

'Nervous?' I say.

'No, course not.'

I look at him.

'Yeah, okay, a bit. Be glad when we can get up there and start playing.'

'Where's Mogs? Isn't he here yet?' Don't tell me he's not coming, please.

'Bog.' Biro nods in the direction of the toilets. 'Nerves. Says he'll be alright as soon as he starts playing.'

The door to the toilet opens and Mogs appears in the doorway; his face is pale and I can see a sheen of sweat on his forehead. He sees us and puts up a hand in a shaky wave then quickly turns around and goes back into the toilet and shuts the door.

'The sooner we get on stage the better.' Biro looks worried.

'Your trousers are cool.' I point at his black and white striped jeans. 'Different.'

He looks down at them and smiles. 'Ace, aren't they? Found them in the loft. They were Dad's.'

An image of Charlie wearing them pops into my head, must be where Biro gets his dress sense from.

'You look different.' Biro has his head on one side as he scrutinises my face.

'Auntie Bridget,' I say, 'Insisted on putting make up on me. I'm her new project. Trying to make me look less like a boy.'

'I like it, just don't go getting those big black eyebrows, will you?'

'No chance. Anyway, I'm going now, see if I can find a good place out in the front to watch you.'

'Okay, Manager.'

I laugh. 'See you later.'

As I turn to leave Biro stops me.

'Before you go?' He looks at Danny and moves me away from him and then lowers his voice.

'What's up?'

'That counselling bloke you're seeing?'

'Adam?'

'Yeah, that's him. You've got that wrong you know, about his mum.'

'What are you on about?'

'About her being dead, she's not dead.'

'She is.'

'She's not. My dad knows *his* dad and he's definitely only been married once.'

'She died years ago.'

'My dad's known him since he was a kid.'

'Your dad must have got it wrong.'

Biro looks annoyed and we stare at each other for a moment and then he shrugs. 'Whatever.' He turns as a grey faced Mogs appears behind him. 'You alright Mogs?'

'Will be,' Mogs says in a shaky voice.

Danny comes over and looks at Mogs with concern.

Biro claps him on the shoulder. 'He'll be fine mate, won't he guys?'

'Yeah,' Danny and I chorus.

'Here, have an extra strong, might make you feel better.' Danny offers Mogs a mint.

Mogs claps a hand over his mouth. 'Don't mention food,' he mumbles through his hand.

'Sorry, mate.'

Biro winks at me. 'Okay, see you later.'

'I'll be watching,' I say and then weave my way through the assorted band members and equipment to the entrance to the bar and something makes me turn and look back. Biro is watching me, I put my hand up in a wave and he waves back unsmiling, then turns away.

Why would Biro think Adam's mum is still alive? It doesn't make any sense; he must have got it wrong.

I slide into the darkened bar and have to stand for a few moments until my eyes adjust to the gloom and I can see properly. Dad brought me up here and showed me around but that was with the lights on; it all looks very different in the dark. The music is so loud it feels as if the floor is pulsating and the music beats its way up through my feet. I want to get to the back of the room away from the stage but I need to stand somewhere where I can get a good view. Tables and chairs are arranged around the edge of the room and the centre is being used as a makeshift dance floor. A group of three leather jacketed guys from college are jumping around in front of the stage and I stand and watch. One of them, tall and skinny with long, floppy hair crashes into a girl watching the band and her drink flies out of her hand. Her meaty looking boyfriend puts his hand on the jumper's chest and shoves him back onto the dance floor and he stumbles and then puts his hand up in apology and staggers away.

I head for the corner of the room where I can stand against the wall, out of the way. I squeeze myself into a space behind the back of a chair and hope that no one stands in front of me. Out of the corner of my eye someone is waving; I look over and then wish that I hadn't. The Clackers are huddled around a small table and Shana is waving frantically at me. I wave back and she stands up and waves both of her arms beckoning me over.

Idiot. Why did I wave back? Now I can't pretend I haven't seen her. I could stay here but I have a feeling she'll come and get me and then she'll really have it in for me. I still haven't grown a pair.

I zigzag my way slowly through the tables, chairs and people, cursing myself for looking her way.

'Hey!' Shana shouts over the noise of the band as I get nearer. 'Come and sit with us.'

'I'll get a drink first,' I shout back. I don't really want a drink, just an excuse not to sit with them. Maybe I can go to the bar and hide.

Shana pulls a stool out from under the table. 'No need, Stacey's at the bar, I'll text her, what do you want?'

'Pint of coke.'

'Okay.' She pulls her phone out and taps out a message.

I sit down on the stool with a sinking heart and say hello to Ellie who's sitting opposite. She doesn't look very happy. It's too much effort to try and talk over the thump of the music so we sit and watch the band.

They're good, but not as good, I think, as Tourists of Reality.

Stacey arrives with the drinks and plonks them on the table, she doesn't look happy and I realise I'm sitting on her seat. Good, that means I can go and stand at the back.

The band finish their set and the next band come on and start to tune up. We're on after them and I feel a little flutter of anticipation.

'Thanks, Stacey, how much do I owe you?'

'S'okay, get me one later.'

I stand up. 'Here, have your seat back.'

'No need,' snaps Shana. 'Stacey can share my chair, half each.' She looks pointedly at Ellie. 'There's probably not enough room on yours, Ellie.'

Shana makes a big show of sitting on half of her seat and Stacey sits next to her. Ellie looks really fed up; why does she want to be friends with these two? I'd rather not have any friends at all.

Shana looks at Ellie with mock concern on her face.

'I just realised that came out all wrong, hun. I wasn't fat shaming you or anything.' She giggles and puts her hand over her mouth. 'Oops, that came out all wrong too. Maybe I should just keep my big mouth shut.' Stacey joins in with the giggling.

I can't bear to look at Ellie so I pick my glass up and take a gulp. It's completely flat.

'Something wrong, hun?'

'Coke's a bit flat, that's all.'

'Hun,' she drops her voice. 'It doesn't matter 'cos we only ever buy one drink.' She pulls a small bottle out of a bag nestled under the table. 'Then top up with our own. Have one of these.' She looks around the room and passes it to me.

I take it off her and she sees my worried expression.

'It's not booze, just fizzy pop.'

I take it off her and open it. It's so dark in here I can't make out what it says on the bottle. I take a sip, very sweet, very fizzy. I take a bigger sip, quite nice.

'Quick, tip it in your coke before someone sees and throws us out.'

I quickly drink half of my flat coke and tip the contents of the bottle in. I take another sip; definitely better than flat coke. I hand the empty bottle to Shana and she shoves it under the table.

'Are this band of yours any good, Josie?' Shana shouts.

'They're not my band.'

'You know what I mean, you're the manager.'

'They are good,' I shout confidently, because they are. 'I think you'll like them.' I take another slurp of my drink; the air is hot and getting hotter.

'Hope so.' Shana smiles. 'Hey, you've nearly drunk that, do you want another one?'

I look at my coke; she's right I have nearly drunk it. I'm about to say yes when Ellie's voice cuts across me.

'No, she doesn't want another one.'

Shana glares at Ellie. 'Wow, Josie, you said that without even opening your mouth.'

Ellie ignores her and turns to me. 'Don't have any more, Josie. They've got alcohol in them.'

'Hardly any at all.' Shana scrabbles around in her bag and pulls out another bottle; she directs a poisonous look at Ellie. 'Party pooper, you're such a dullard sometimes.'

'No,' I put my hand up. 'I've got enough here, thanks anyway.'

'Okay, hun, whatever.'

I take a big slurp of my drink, it doesn't taste like alcohol.

'Sure you don't want another one of these?' Shana reaches under the table and wiggles the bottle at me.

'No, this is fine,' I say, taking another swallow, 'Just fine.'

Shana smiles her sly smile and the band begins to play. The drummer is banging an almost hypnotic beat and the dance floor fills with people. There's a party atmosphere in the room and I feel myself jigging in my seat to the music. Shana and Stacey stand up waving their arms around and doing cute little wiggles and a lot of the guys are looking at them. I wish I had their confidence.

Ellie hasn't moved and I catch her eye and she gives me a reluctant smile.

'Cheer up,' I mouth to her over the music but her expression doesn't change.

And then the music dies and Tourists of Reality arrive on the stage. My stomach does a lazy roll and my mouth feels dry. I'm excited and nervous for them and I cross my fingers under the table. They look all *musiciany* and serious, tuning their guitars as if they do gigs every day of the week, but I know how nervous they are. Mogs still looks grey and Biro keeps swallowing because I can see his Adam's apple bobbing; he always does that when he's nervous. Danny looks cheerful, he's already getting admiring glances from plenty of girls in the audience and is lapping it up.

'Hello Frogham.' Biro has the microphone, it squeals with feedback and he stops and adjusts the volume. The room is silent, my mouth goes even dryer so I drain the rest of my drink.

'We're Tourists of Reality and we're going to play a

mash up of old and new.' There are shouts of *get on with it* and *you're not fucking Elton John* and I start to worry then that it's all going to go horribly wrong.

Biro takes the hint and nods at Mogs and Danny and I hold my breath as they start to play.

And they're brilliant; absolutely amazing. Yes, I am a bit biased but they are the best of the night. The serious rocker types stand and watch Mogs playing, they don't jig, or dance, they just watch with serious expressions on their faces. Mogs sounds even more amazing than in rehearsal and he doesn't even look up; just his curtain of hair bobbing slightly as he plays. Biro and Danny's voices meld together and although Danny has to move around a bit so the true rockers don't see he's not really playing, he looks the part.

The floor in front of the stage is full; people bouncing and fists pumping the air. I climb up onto my chair to see over their heads. I feel a bit wobbly and am about to get down when Shana pulls her chair next to mine and stands up next to me.

'They're amaze,' she shouts in my ear, clutching hold of my arm. 'Aren't you proud!'

'I am!' I shout, lightheaded with the excitement of it all.

Shana puts her mouth closer to my ear. 'Don't you just wish you were up on stage with them, hun?'

And that's when it all goes horribly wrong.

Chapter 14

Josie

I slowly open my eyes and stare at the ceiling. I turn my head to the side to look at my alarm clock to see what time it is and this is when my skull moves but somehow my brain doesn't. The pain is unbearable and excruciating and tears spring to my eyes. I lie absolutely still and wait for the pain to subside before I attempt to focus on the clock. I think it might say 8:37 but I'm not completely sure because I'm having trouble processing thoughts right now.

I slowly close my eyes; if I don't move at all I can go back to sleep. I don't want to wake up.

I open my eyes and slowly move my head to look at the clock; my brain wobbles but not quite so much as before; 11:30. After several minutes I work out that I must have fallen asleep again and I try to work out how many hours I've been asleep but the effort is too much. I put my elbows on the bed and slowly push myself upright. Not so bad. I'm still wearing the clothes I went out in last night minus my jeans and boots.

Actually, I think sitting up was a mistake, I feel sick. I swivel my eyes frantically around the room without moving my head which hurts much more than I thought it would. I know I won't make it to the bathroom in time. I spy my Minions waste bin sitting next to my desk. Sorry Kevin, it looks like it's going to be you. I slide out of bed onto the floor trying to move my head as little as possible and commando crawl on my elbows, dragging myself to the bin. I was wrong about feeling better than the first time I woke up, the pain is just as bad as it was before, in fact I think I might actually be dying.

I manage to reach the bin and I clasp my hands around the rim and hang my head and vomit what feels like the entire contents of my body into it. There's a whimpering noise and after a while my brain works out that it's me. I wipe a shaking hand across my mouth and almost vomit again at the fetid remnants of last night's burger. Gross. I lay on the floor, exhausted, with my arms still wrapped tightly around Kevin the Minion when I hear a gentle tap at the door. I know it'll be Dad, I can't believe he's waited this long to see why I'm not up.

'Sweetheart?' The door opens slowly and Dad tentatively pokes his head around it.

'Oh, Dad.' I burst into tears. 'I'm dying.'

Dad sits down on the floor next to me and rubs my back as I sob.

'It's okay sweetheart, it's just a hangover, you'll feel better by tomorrow.'

'Aren't you angry with me?' I blubber through the snot and tears.

'Well, I wish you hadn't done it but I don't think you'll be in a hurry to do it again will you?'

I wouldn't have done it at all if I'd known there was alcohol in that fizzy drink. One drink surely wouldn't make me so drunk, would it? No, of course it wouldn't. I knew that coke tasted peculiar, Stacey must have spiked it when she was at the bar, no wonder it was so flat.

I cry even louder and Dad puts his arm around me.

'Come on, we've all been there, it's not the end of the world. Get back into bed. Do you think you could eat a piece of toast?'

'Don't mention food!' I wail.

'Okay, okay.' He gently pulls me to my feet as if I'm an invalid and guides me over to the bed and I flop onto the mattress and crawl underneath the duvet. Dad tucks me in and I hear him pick the bin up.

'Have a good sleep and you'll feel better.'

'Dad?'

'Yep?'

'Sorry.'

I wake and the room in is darkness. I turn over gingerly to find that my headache has evolved into a rhythmic, steady, thump. I feel slightly better and manage to sit up without feeling sick. I have a raging thirst and surprisingly, I feel hungry too.

I get out of bed and yank my dressing gown from the back of the door and pull it on. My legs feel wobbly and my head feels like it might fall off my neck and roll away but I manage to stagger down the stairs and into the lounge. Dad's sitting watching the football but he jumps up when he sees me.

'How are you feeling?'

'Better,' I say. 'Just going to get a drink.'

'No, you sit down, I'll get it.'

I sit down on the sofa and pull the furry throw from the sofa arm over me. Skipper is watching me from his normal spot by the fire and if I thought it was possible, I'd say he looks disgusted with me.

I'm disgusted with me.

Dad comes back in with a glass of water and hands it to me with two paracetamol. I gulp it down without stopping thinking that water never, ever tasted so good.

'Toast?' Dad asks hopefully.

'Please.'

He goes back out to the kitchen and I hear the sound of cupboards opening and plates clattering. Skipper walks hesitantly towards me and I put my hand out to him and he sniffs it, then gives it a hesitant lick.

'Here you are.' Dad comes in and thrusts a plate of toast at me. 'I can do you more if you want it.'

I'm suddenly starving and I bolt the toast down and follow it with another glass of water; I don't think I'll ever get rid of this thirst.

'Do you want to talk about it?'

I nod. 'But first, tell me how I got home, I can't even remember.'

Dad sits down on the sofa next to me. 'Your friend Biro rang me, said he thought I ought to come and pick you up because you weren't feeling well.'

'Oh God.'

'When I got there you were asleep in the room at the back where the bands get changed, couldn't get any sense out of you at all.' I can see the worry on Dad's face; how frightening it must have been for him.

'I'm so sorry, Dad, really sorry.' I think I'm going to cry again.

'Look, don't get upset. You're alright and that's the main thing, I'm just surprised that you drank alcohol – you always say you don't even like the taste of it.'

So I tell him about the alcopop thing and how I

think Stacey probably spiked my drink. How dumb am I that I didn't even notice? Dad looks more and more angry by the minute.

'Think I'll be ringing her parents and having a word about that young lady. And I'm surprised that Ellie hangs around with people like that.'

'No, don't, Dad. It won't happen again because I won't be so stupid and gullible. I just thought she was being friendly.'

Dad looks a bit calmer.

'Okay. Don't know what's up with these kids, why do they have to be so spiteful? I sat in your room watching you for hours, making sure you didn't vomit and choke to death on it.'

I look at him in shock.

'I didn't know what you'd drunk, or how much.'

I shake my head, big mistake; brain shake.

'Anyway, no harm done, lucky you've got a sensible friend in Biro.'

If he's still my friend.

'Your phone's been beeping away like mad. I put it on charge in the kitchen for you.'

Oh God. I need more toast before I have the strength to look at my phone. Dad reads my mind.

'Some more?' He picks the plate up.

'Please.'

Dad goes out into the kitchen and I snuggle under the throw and wallow; a wet nose nudges my hand and I look down to see Skipper's little face staring at me. I put my hand on his head and stroke his ears. I pull him up onto the sofa and nuzzle my face in his furry little neck.

'You won't let me down, will you Skip?'

He gazes at me and sniffs the air.

Rank. I bet I smell absolutely rank.

An overwhelming feeling of disgust and shame swamps me and I fight back tears.

No use crying now.

I put on clean pyjamas after my shower and wrap my dressing gown tightly around me. I'm feeling more human now. Before I got into the shower, I brushed my teeth and when I caught sight of my reflection in the mirror, I frightened myself. The mascara so skilfully applied by Auntie Bridget was all over my face and my hair was sticking up in tufts. I looked like a zombie.

I comb my wet hair and rub some cream on my face; a bit better though my eyes look puffy. Probably all the blubbing.

I open the window in my bedroom, it's freezing out but I need to rid the room of the smell of vomit. My stomach churns just thinking about it. Kevin the waste bin is in back in his place, cleaned and washed by Dad and I notice he's changed the sheets too.

I sit down on the bed and prepare myself to look at my phone. Dad said it had been beeping and it's all charged up but I haven't looked at it. I've been deliberately putting it off.

I pick it up carefully as if it might explode in my hands and tap the messages icon. There are four WhatsApp messages from Biro:

You okay mate?
You up yet?
Ring me when you get up.
You avoiding me?

Surprisingly there's also one from Ellie:

Hi, hope you're okay. Sorry about those cows last night, I had NOTHING to do with it. X

It's Ellie's message that gets to me; it reminds of when we used to text all the time, when we were friends. I feel like crying again but stop myself. Crying won't help.

I can't face speaking to Biro so I text him:

Just got up, awful hangover (sad face emoji) feeling too ill to talk, see you tomoz.

He replies almost instantly.

How much did you have FFS? Have you seen FB yet?'

Oh God.

No, I'm not on FB.

Biro replies: *Forgot you're a social media retard. Will WhatsApp you the clip. You need to see it. It's all over FB and someone's even put it on YouTube.*

Seconds later a WhatsApp message comes through and a video starts to download. Thanks Biro. I thought you were my friend.

Will look later, I message. *Feeling ill so going to bed*

I take my dressing gown off and crawl underneath the duvet.

Kill me now.

Chapter 15

Josie

I thought about pretending to be ill and not going to college; stay at home and wallow in misery. But then I thought no, *make an effort* as Mum always used to say, face up to things, stop hiding and hoping everything will somehow magically disappear.

Yeah, *face up to things,* says a little voice, *as if; you haven't even got the guts to watch the clip.*

Realistically, I can't pretend to be ill forever so I might as well just get it over with. I'd studied myself in the bathroom mirror before I left home and spent ages practising my *I'm not bothered* expression. It was pathetic and I couldn't even convince myself, so no one else is going to believe me.

Dad drops me off in the college car park and as I wave goodbye to him, I look around to see who's about. I usually get the bus but Dad offered as he's working from home and honestly, I didn't want to get on the bus in case there was someone on there who'd seen me on Facebook. I'm just delaying it, I know. I wish I could time travel and it was next year and all this was a distant memory.

When I think things like that, I know how truly

weird I am.

I spot the familiar lanky figure of Biro ahead of me sauntering through the gates and I speed up and try to catch him up and shout his name.

'Yo, mate.' He turns and smiles and stops and waits for me. I'm surprised he doesn't seem annoyed with me. I was sure he'd be seething.

'Hiya.' My face is hot and I realise I'm going to have to spend the entire day with a beetroot complexion.

'Did you watch that clip I sent you?' he says with a big grin.

'No.'

'Look,' I stop and grab his arm. 'I'm really sorry about Saturday, I'm sorry I ruined your gig and my only defence is that Shana spiked my drink. I'll get you another gig, I promise, and I won't ruin it next time.' I just hope Dad can sweet talk his mate at the Vic again.

Biro looks at me incredulously and then he starts to laugh, I mean really laugh, and I stand there watching him. Eventually he stops laughing and puts his arm around me and pulls me alongside him and we start walking again. I quicken my step to keep up with his lanky strides. I'm so relieved he's still my friend although I could kill him for finding it so funny.

'Mate,' he says, as we walk through the college entrance, 'You really need to watch the clip.'

Just my luck, the first class of the day and the Clackers are also in it. Biro went off to his class and said he'd see me later and when I asked him if he'd forgiven me, he got all mysterious and said I needed to watch the clip. I could hit him sometimes, why can't he just put me out of my misery and tell me what an idiot I made of myself and we can move on and forget it. I'll force him to tell me at lunchtime, at least I only have one class to get through this morning.

I was drunk and I don't remember a lot of things but I do remember getting up on stage and grabbing the microphone off a gobsmacked Biro. I remember demanding that the band play *Wonderwall* so I could sing it.

Yeah, told you it was bad. Wonderwall? Really? A song from my Dad's generation and I can't even sing either. This is why I don't want to look at it, I don't need to see how bad it was, *I know*. No wonder Biro couldn't stop laughing.

The first thing I notice when I walk into class is Ellie sitting on her own; she's at the opposite side of the room from Shana and Stacey. I look at her in surprise and she beckons me over. I walk over and I can feel Shana and Stacey's eyes watching me.

'Hi.' I flop down in the chair next to Ellie.

'Hi, are you okay?'

'I'm okay.'

'I was really worried about you, I messaged you but then wondered if you'd changed your number when I didn't get a reply.'

'Sorry I didn't reply, was feeling a bit rough.' I laugh nervously. I feel bad that I didn't message her now. Am I going to spend the rest of my life feeling guilty for everything I do or don't do? I think I am.

'Just wanted you to know that I had nothing to do with it, nothing to do with *them*.' She glares across the room at Shana and Stacey who are watching us with interest.

'Aren't you friends with them anymore?'

'Friends?' snorts Ellie. 'They're not friends, they're bitches, don't know why it's taken me so long to see it.

How is spiking someone's drink even supposed to be funny? They can both fuck right off.' She stares directly at them when she says it and I can see by their shocked faces that they've got the message.

'Ellie...?' I start to say but I never finish because the tutor comes in and starts handing out our marked essays from last week. I look over at Shana and Stacey expecting to see them laughing and sniggering at me but they're not; they look subdued and can't quite meet my eye. In spite of my misery I feel a little spark of happiness; Ellie and I are friends again.

Ellie slides a note along the desk to me and I slide it under my essay but I've seen what it says and the little spark goes out; *do you know you're on YouTube?*

There's no avoiding it. Man up Josie Sparkes, face the music.

When the class ends and everyone files out of the door, I stay seated and Ellie stays too. I pick up the piece of paper.

'Biro told me. I haven't watched it. Too embarrassed.'

'You haven't watched it?' Ellie looks at me in disbelief.

'No. Can't bear to.' I will *not* cry.

'But, Josie.' Ellie is already pulling her mobile out of her bag. 'You were *amazing.*'

I've watched it several times; I think amazing is an overstatement but it's not the horror film I was expecting. I don't look too bad considering I fell asleep in the changing room straight afterwards and I didn't slur the words in spite of being absolutely mortal. My voice isn't good, never has been, but it *is* in tune. But it's not that, apparently, that's amazing. It's the *attitude*.

The strutting, obnoxious, skinny little girl belting out Wonderwall on stage is nothing like me and I have no idea where that alter ego comes from. It must have been the alcohol that gave me that confidence – there must be a part of me that's really like that and even though I've watched it over and over I still can't believe it.

I can't believe the girl strutting around, shouting at the crowd and practically spitting the words out is *me*. Where did all that anger and passion come from? And why Wonderwall? I don't even *like* the song. I knew all of the words too, Dad's constant playing of it must have seared itself onto my brain. There's no doubt the crowd liked it as everyone is singing along and I can almost taste the atmosphere from the clip. Biro is playing the keyboard and singing along and he looks ecstatic and Danny and Mogs are giving it their all too.

'See? Told you it was amazing. I never knew you could sing like that.'

'Nor did I.'

It's not just me on YouTube, someone filmed Tourists of Reality's entire set and that *is* amazing; next time they play they'll be queuing up to see them. I'm so relieved that I didn't ruin it for them.

'Are you going to the canteen for lunch?' I stand up and hook my bag over my shoulder.

Ellie's face reddens. 'Wasn't going to bother. If I sit on my own those two cows will just come and sit with me and start the fat jokes.'

'Sit with us,' I say.

'Won't Biro mind?'

'Course he won't, any friend of mine is a friend of his.'

Ellie's face lights up. 'Okay,' she says, getting up and

linking her arm through mine. 'Lead on Sparky.'

I laugh and it already feels like the last couple of years are melting away; Ellie always used to call me Sparky when we were best friends.

I get the odd strange look or double take on the way to the canteen but I know now that I didn't make a complete idiot of myself so I can live with it and I don't hear anyone laughing so maybe I can even enjoy it a bit.

Ellie and I join Biro who's sitting at our usual table in the corner. He doesn't look a bit surprised to see Ellie.

'Hi Ellie, how's it going?' he asks with a smile.

'All good,' she says. Did she just blush slightly or did I imagine it?

I sit down opposite Biro and tell him that I've seen the clip. He smiles a big cheesy grin from ear to ear.

'Loads of hits on YouTube, it's gone mental…had a phone call from the geezer at the Vic, he wants us to play again.'

'He rang *you*?' I ask in disbelief.

'Yep. He says he likes the idea of getting someone on stage out of the audience at the end of the set; thought it was a good idea, a bit different. He didn't seem to know you were our manager.' Biro looks puzzled.

I decide to confess and tell him that it was Dad who got them the gig. Biro doesn't seem the least bit bothered and I feel better for telling him, I'm not good at lying.

'Got to say, Josie, thought I knew you but you surprised me. You'd give Liam Gallagher a run for his money.' Biro stares at me and shakes his head.

'Who?'

'Philistine. Anyway, you've got Ellie here to thank

me for ringing your Dad. She came and told me what those two had done.'

I look at Ellie in surprise.

'I thought it was strange how you fell asleep straight after our set.'

He stops talking and looks up as Shana and Stacey noisily make themselves known. They're standing at the end of our table, trays in hand.

'Mind if we join you?' simpers Shana, fluttering her eyelashes.

''Yeah, we do mind, actually. We're choosy who we sit with.' Biro barks at them.

'Okay, no need to be rude.' Shana sniffs. 'Come on Stacey, let's go find some people to sit with who aren't losers.' The walk off in their flat ballet pumped, cutesy way. The three of us look at each other and burst out laughing. And it feels so good to laugh.

I watch as Shana and Stacey find an empty table by the door and sit down, sour expressions on their faces. I suddenly have a feeling of being watched, and I guess that someone has seen the YouTube clip and is connecting the dots. I look around but no one is looking at me, it's my imagination. Get over yourself, Sparkes, you're not that famous.

A figure passing the window catches my eye and I see Adam hurrying across the car park and seeing him reminds me. His mother. What Biro said about his mother not being dead. I need to clear this up with Biro; I open my mouth to ask him and then close it again. Biro's deep in conversation with Ellie and I don't want to interrupt them, their eyes are locked on each other and they seem engrossed. Could my two best friends be getting it together?

I smile to myself and pick up my drink; it's not

important, it'll keep, I'll ask him another day.

Chapter 16

Josie

I'm early again. It's getting to be a habit.

Today I'm looking forward to telling Adam about the gig, the drink spiking part is not good but the rest of it is. It'll be good to have a positive conversation and not be negative all the time. The last couple of days a few people have come up to me and said how great Tourists of Reality are and some even commented on my singing. A few months ago, I'd have thought they were mocking me but now I'm starting to take people at face value. I shouldn't assume that everyone is like Shana and Stacey. And if they are mocking me, so what? It can only hurt me if I let it.

I stretch my legs out and settle back into the chair. This office could do with a good dust and you'd think they'd chuck the out of date calendars out. I wouldn't like to have to work in here for any length of time, it's so far away from the main part of the college that it feels quite cut off. Adam should complain and demand a better room.

Listen to me; demand a better room. Slow down Sparkes, who do you think you are? Don't get carried away with yourself.

A little cloud floats by and darkens my mood for a moment; I hope we don't have to talk about Mum again today.

'Hi!' Adam's arrived and he breezes in and flings the door shut and then settles himself in the chair, long legs sprawling. I gently bend my knees and pull my legs in and tuck my feet under the chair. Not enough room for both of us to have our legs stretched out. Not without touching. He's looking a bit flushed, like he's been running or outside in the cold. He is *so* handsome. I wish I were older.

'So let's see where we got to last time.' Adam rifles through his notebook, frowning. I feel annoyed that he has to refresh his memory, can't he remember? Get a grip, Sparkes, you're just another client.

'Ah, yes, here we are. So, do you think it helped talking about your mother in our last session?' It was too much to hope that we wouldn't have to talk about Mum again; my mood starts to deflate.

'Yes, I think it did.' This is a lie; it didn't help, I just felt disloyal and guilty and I'd rather just forget about it and pretend Mum wasn't having an affair.

'Good. It's best to get things out in the open where you can make sense of them. Us humans are very complex. To you your mother was warm, loving and totally loyal but other people would say she was also a liar and a cheat.'

'No she wasn't!' I burst out. How dare he speak about her like that!

Adam puts his hand up. 'Josie, *I'm* not saying that. I'm simply saying that other people may perceive her like that from her behaviour. Everyone has their own point of reference. None of us like to think of our parents as not being perfect but they're only human and everyone makes mistakes.'

I swallow down my anger and nod. I have to stop this talking about her. Now.

'The gig went really well.' I try to sound upbeat and I stretch my lips into a fake smile.

'That's great.'

'Even better than I imagined. Tourists of Reality were brilliant, they've been asked back to do another gig.'

'Really? That's amazing!'

'I know! The guys are over the moon, they deserve it though, they're so good. I think they're going to collect quite a following.'

'Fantastic! And you have to take some credit because they couldn't have done it without you. It must have felt good watching them on stage.'

'It did. Loads of people were on their feet singing along, it was the best night ever.' Apart from the spiked drink.

'Good.' Adam smiles that lovely crinkly eyed smile that makes me feel so good and I think why spoil it by telling him about the drink spiking? I know I'm supposed to be honest but it's done with now, I'm over it, no harm done as Dad says. And, it makes me look like a stupid, immature kid who doesn't even know what she's doing.

'Okay?' Adam is still smiling at me.

'Yes,' I nod. 'I'm fine.'

'Nothing else to tell me?'

'No.' I say hesitantly.

'You didn't join in with the band at all?' He's outright grinning now and I realise that he knows.

'Sorry,' he says, running a hand through his hair. 'That's not fair of me. I overheard some students talking about a clip on YouTube and I put two and two together and so I had a look.'

Will he know I was drunk? I think back; it's a completely different me on YouTube but I don't look drunk, maybe a bit demented but not drunk.

'Oh?' What will he think? I suddenly realise that it's really important to me what Adam thinks.

'I hardly recognised you, you didn't look one bit like the frightened young girl that walked into this office a few weeks ago.'

'No?' I can feel myself starting to grin, it's catching.

'No, you looked like a gutsy, grown up version of her, a confident young woman. You were incredible.'

I feel myself starting to blush. My God. He called me incredible.

'And you need to learn how to take a compliment because I'm sure you're going to be getting a lot more of them in the future.'

Does he mean from him? Of course not, don't be so dumb.

I nod my head stupidly and smile and curse myself for being so lame.

'So. How are you getting on with your Dad now?'

'Really well,' I say, relieved that he's changed the subject. 'But we've always got on, we never really argue.'

'He's always supportive?'

'Always.'

I remember Biro's comment about Adam's Mum; he must have remarried a long time ago and I open my mouth to ask him and then close it again. If I say anything, he'll know that I've been talking about him and I don't think he'd like it if he knew I'd repeated what he told me. I'll look like a stupid little girl who can't keep her mouth shut.

'That's good. What does he think about your rendition of Wonderwall?'

I start to laugh. I showed Dad the clip last night and he was gobsmacked. Wanted to know how I knew all of the words and I said they must have soaked in to my brain somehow when he used to play his Oasis albums all of the time. He kept replaying the clip and sat watching it, shaking his head and saying, *I can't believe it*. He loved it though, said he was going to send it to Auntie Bridget and Uncle Ralph.

'He loved it, he's an Oasis fan.'

'He's proud of you?'

'Yes,' I say after a moment as I think about it. 'I think he is.' It's a nice feeling, Dad being proud of me instead of constantly worrying about me.

'He's right to be proud of you. I'm proud of you, too.'

I laugh, not knowing what to say.

'I can see I'll have to be careful in future, now that I've seen that little wildcat inside you on the stage.'

'Yes, you'd better watch out.'

'Oh, I will.' Adam laughs.

'Or who knows what I'll do.'

'Who knows what else might be hidden underneath that calm exterior?'

'Who knows?' I raise an eyebrow and try to affect a mysterious expression.

And then it hits me, we're *flirting*.

I don't know whether the same thought occurs to Adam because he looks down at his notebook with a smile and ruffles through it and the next minute we're talking about coping mechanisms for my exams.

We were though; flirting. Most definitely. I hug the

141

thought to me as we continue with the rest of the session and look forward to reliving it later. Time goes too quickly and before I know it the session's over and it's time to leave.

'See you on Friday,' I say as I gather my bag and stand up.

'Have a good week, Josie.'

'I will.'

'And no more balancing on chairs to get a better view.'

I laugh. 'I won't!'

I come out of the room and practically skip along the corridor, feeling light hearted and happy. Is this how most people my age feel most of the time? Is this how I *should* feel? I know I have a silly smile on my face but I can't help it. I didn't want the session to end, it was so lovely talking to Adam and having normal conversation (well, after I'd managed to shut him up about Mum) and there was definitely some flirting going on – or was I imagining it after all? I've never flirted before so I'm not sure. I'm probably just flattering myself but I don't care, I really like Adam even though I know he's far too old for me and nothing will ever come of it. It's not a crush though, I'm not a silly teenager.

Well, I am a teenager, but I'm definitely not silly. Anyway, I'm not going to analyse it, I'm feeling happier that I've felt for a long time and that's good enough for me. I turn the corner into the assembly hall and weave my way across the room through the rows of chairs facing the stage.

Hang on though, something Adam said is niggling, but what is it?

Nothing, says a little voice, you're just looking for a

reason to spoil everything.

Am I?

No, I'm not.

I know what it is. Adam last words to me were *no more balancing on chairs*, but I never told him about that.

And it wasn't on the clip.

So how did he know?

I feel a thrill of excitement surge through me.

Was he there *watching* me?

Chapter 17

Josie

There's a new confidence in the band since the gig; they thought they were good, but now they know it. Biro has taught Danny three basic chords on the guitar and somehow Danny is playing them in the right places, at the right time. He's overjoyed and I've noticed he's started doing a flamboyant sort of arm wave when he hits the last chord.

I raided the cupboards at home and have bought along drinks and crisps for a break. I don't need to be here really because there's not a lot of managing to do. I help move the tables and chairs out of the way and then move them back at the end and the rest of the time I just sit and watch them. I just love being here though.

'Can't tempt you Josie?' Biro holds the microphone out to me. 'Another rendition of Wonderwall?'

'Definitely not. One night only, I'm afraid.'

'Shame, was something else, you should have been there.' Biro winks at me to show he's joking.

'You *were* great, Josie.' Danny gives me a smile. 'You could be our singer you know, you've got a better voice than me or Biro.'

'No, I'm happy as manager, thanks.'

Biro looks a bit annoyed at Danny's comment and I quickly change the subject.

'Did Jason give you a date for the next gig?'

'Yeah, two weeks tomorrow. We've got the best spot too, last on.'

'We need to sort a diary out,' I say. 'Because there's an open band night here in the college in April and a lot of the pubs in town have new band nights, usually on Sunday nights.'

'Cool,' Biro says. 'You've been busy.'

I have. I can't rely on Dad to keep getting gigs for the band and I am supposed to be the manager so I rang around most of the pubs in town. A few of them had heard of Tourists of Reality so there must be some sort of band grapevine.

'They get booked up pretty quickly so we need to be organised.'

'Yes, boss.' Biro salutes. 'You should ask your mate to come along.' He says it casually but he's not fooling me.

'Ellie?'

'Yeah,' he says, nonchalantly. 'Unless she's out with her boyfriend or something.'

Ellie and I have seen a lot of each other this week, we have a lot of classes together anyway but it's nice to be friends again. It's made me realise how much I've missed spending time with her. I won't lose her friendship again, I know that. If we seem to be drifting apart, I'll say something instead of curling up in my shell and pushing everyone away and feeling sorry for myself.

'I'll ask her. I don't know if she's got a boyfriend.'

I know she hasn't; I'm just winding Biro up, which

makes a change from him winding me up. Funnily enough I was going to ask if she wanted to come but I thought I'd better check with the band first.

'Is that her with the big hair?' Mogs peers over at me squinting; he should really wear his glasses because he can't see a thing without them.

I laugh. 'That's her.'

Ellie's hair *is* big; a gorgeous, bouncy mass of black curls. She hates it of course, is always trying to straighten it and tame it while everyone else is trying to curl theirs and get some volume into it. Except me, my hair is so short it couldn't be any more low maintenance.

Biro is studying Mogs with interest. 'Didn't know you knew Ellie.'

Mogs shrug. 'I don't.'

Oh my, Biro's got it bad.

'Guys!' I drum roll on the table with my hands. 'We're wasting valuable time, get on with rehearsing,' I say in a stern voice. 'Before I get my whip out.'

The rehearsal went really well and Biro and I are waiting in the car park for his Dad, Charlie, to pick us up.

'You seem happier.' Biro is giving me an appraising look.

'I am. I think talking to Adam is really helping. Weird, really, because I couldn't see how talking could possibly help but it has.'

'Good.' Biro stares at me a bit too long and I start to feel uncomfortable.

'What?'

'Nothing.'

'Then why are you looking at me like that?' I sound

annoyed. I am annoyed.

'You know Adam's just a counsellor, right?'

'What's that supposed to mean?'

'Nothing.' Biro shrugs.

'If you've got something to say, just say it.'

Biro looks at me in surprise. 'Whoa. Defensive or what.'

'No, I'm not.'

'You are. I'm just saying he's a counsellor, it's his job.'

'I know that.' I punch Biro playfully on the arm. 'I'm not some stupid kid you know, I haven't got the hots for him or anything.'

Biro looks at me for a bit longer then turns away.

'Come on, Pa's here.' He picks up his guitar and strides towards Charlie's battered mini. I have to jog to match his giant steps.

'Hello chick.'

'Hello, Charlie.' I say as I clamber into the back seat. How brave I am, no more Mr Birowski.

Biro hands me his guitar and folds himself into the front seat then pushes the seat back as far as possible nearly cutting my legs off in the process. We zoom off before I've even had a chance to put my seatbelt on, I try to juggle the guitar and seatbelt but soon give up; way too much effort.

'Christ, Pa, when you going to get a car I can fit into?'

'There's always the bus.'

Biro huffs and looks out of the window.

'Good rehearsal?' asks Charlie.

'Yeah.'

What's the matter with Biro? He's my best friend but he seems to have a problem with Adam; he's taken a dislike to him and he's never even met him. Maybe I've been talking about Adam too much. I told him how we laughed about my YouTube fame. Now I think about it, maybe I do talk about him a lot. Is Biro jealous that I've got another friend? I didn't think Biro was like that. I resolve not to talk about Adam anymore, Biro's probably sick of hearing about him.

But Biro is wrong.

Adam is *not* just my counsellor.

I let myself in the front door and the smell of the curry we had for tea is still lingering in the air. It was one of Dad's special currys; basically, anything left in the fridge gets flung in with whatever spices and chillies are available. Tonight's was pretty fiery; my lips are still tingling.

The house feels warm and cosy and I'm relieved to be out of Charlie's mini. Biro can be a right pig sometimes; he moaned like mad when he had to get out of the car so I could get out of the back seat. I said to him, you should have let me sit in the front if it's such a problem and he said it's okay for you, you're practically a midget anyway. I could have hit him, I may be small but even so I was practically scrunched up into a ball on the way home, he must have known.

I take my coat off and hang it up and for a moment I think that Dad must have gone to bed, it's so quiet. I look at my watch; he wouldn't go to bed at a quarter past ten on a Friday night, he always waits for me to come home; says he can't sleep until he knows I'm safe. I look in the lounge and the lights are on but the TV is off and Skipper is fast asleep, curled up cosily on the sofa. His feet are twitching, he's chasing dream rabbits.

And then I hear the murmur of Dad's voice from

upstairs, I stand and listen for a moment. I can't hear what he's saying but it's a one-sided conversation, so he must be on the phone. I breathe a sigh of relief and then wonder what I was so afraid of, where did I think he was? What did I think had happened to him?

I was suddenly frightened he was going to be taken away from me, like Mum.

I go into the kitchen and get myself a glass of water to take to bed, I have work tomorrow but I don't mind, I enjoy it. Not the job; that's beyond boring but I like Louise and Uncle Ralph is funny, even though he doesn't mean to be. Louise took me downstairs to the print room last week and we watched Bert and Lev as they printed Saturday's Herald. It was a noisy clatter, clatter, but sort of mesmerising. The paper whizzes off the press so fast and then Lev grabs big thick wedges of it and feeds it into another machine and they come out folded and ready to sell. Bert didn't seem to do much; he stood watching the press, frowning and blowing his cheeks out and just twiddled a few knobs now and again. We didn't stay for too long because Louise says Lev gets a bit twitchy around women and he did start muttering something about *Dagmar no like* so we went back upstairs. It was more or less finish time then and Dad was waiting outside in the car so I had to go, but she said she'd tell me what she meant about Lev being twitchy tomorrow.

I go upstairs and see the door to Dad's bedroom ajar and I'm about to pop my head around the door and wave goodnight at him when something about the conversation stops me.

I'm eavesdropping.

'I know,' Dad says. 'But I don't want to upset her.'

Dad is quiet for a moment as whoever's on the other

end of the phone speaks.

'She doesn't need to know, she's been through enough.'

I hold my breath.

'I don't want to tell her. I don't even know why we're having this conversation. I don't want to talk about how *he* nearly destroyed us.'

Then silence again.

'Yeah, Ralph, she might be old enough but some things are better kept quiet. What's the point now? I can't see how telling her is going to help. She doesn't need to know.'

I step through the doorway and Dad looks up at me in alarm.

'What don't I need to know, Dad?'

Chapter 18

Josie

Dad stares at me open mouthed, I can hear Uncle Ralph's squawking coming out of the phone.

'Ring you later.' Dad stabs his finger on the *end call* button and slowly puts the phone down on the bedside table.

'Well?' I demand, hands on hips.

'It's not what you think.'

'You don't know what I think.'

'It's nothing worth mentioning.'

'Who's HE?'

The fight seems to go out of Dad and he seems to deflate in front of me and his shoulders slump. He suddenly looks old and tired as he rubs his eyes and then drags his hand through his hair.

'Just give me a minute.' He takes a deep, shuddering breath and closes his eyes. I wait. I'll stand here until he tells me but I wish he'd hurry up. He looks so dejected that I'm starting to feel bad about the way I'm speaking to him.

'Why are you sweating, Dad?' He's got beads of sweat on his forehead and it's not *that* warm in here, in fact it's not warm at all.

He looks up at me and I notice how grey he looks. He gives a shaky smile.

'Wasn't feeling too great so I came up for a lie down and then your Uncle Ralph rang.'

'In what way don't you feel great?'

Dad doesn't answer and shakes his head and wraps his arms tightly around his chest. I watch in mounting horror as he slumps forward over his knees.

'Dad! What's wrong? Tell me!'

'You'd better call your uncle Ralph,' he says in a whisper. 'I think I'm having a heart attack.'

'I should have called an ambulance!' I shout from the back seat of Uncle Ralph's car.

'It'll be fine, pet. If you'd called an ambulance you'd still be waiting now.' Auntie Bridget puts her arm around me and gives me a comforting squeeze but I can't take my eyes off Dad. He's sitting in the front passenger seat next to Uncle Ralph and is sweating even more now and he looks so frightened. I'm so scared and I keep repeating *please don't die* over and over in my head. It's all my fault, I shouldn't have been so horrible to him.

'Slow down, Ralph,' barks Auntie Bridget. 'Because if Robbie hasn't had a heart attack, you're going to give him one with your mad driving.'

Uncle Ralph ignores her; he's hunched over the steering wheel with his nose practically pressed against the windscreen. I didn't think it was possible for anyone to drive so fast. When I rang him, it seemed like I'd hardly put the phone down before he burst through the front door and raced up the stairs. He left the key in the front door and would have driven off and left the door wide open if Auntie Bridget hadn't stopped him. They only live ten minutes away but I'm sure they did the journey in like, sixty seconds.

The gigantic outline of Frogham Infirmary looms out of the darkness and Uncle Ralph slams his foot on the brake as we screech around the corner into the hospital car park. Auntie Bridget and I slide across the seats and I squash her into the door, stretching our seat belts to the limit.

'Where's A&E?' Uncle Ralph's voice is all wobbly.

'Straight on down here then it's on the left, shouts Auntie Bridget. 'And slow DOWN.'

Ignoring her, Uncle Ralph speeds up even more and we hurtle along the road then career sharply to the left on what feels like two wheels. We weave our way through the car park and then stop so suddenly that I nearly head butt the back of Uncle Ralph's seat even though I have a seat belt on.

'You can't stop here!' shouts Auntie Bridget. We're right outside the doors of A&E, with two wheels on the pavement.

Uncle Ralph ignores her and already has his door open and is jumping out and racing over to the A&E entrance. Auntie Bridget and I clamber out and by the time I get round to Dad's door Uncle Ralph has reappeared with a wheelchair.

He yanks Dad's door open and pushes the wheelchair closer to the car.

'I'm not getting in that, I can walk,' Dad says in a weak voice.

'You're not walking.' Uncle Ralph leans into the car and attempts to pull Dad out. 'Mind out the way, Josie.'

'What do you think you're doing?'

'Helping you.'

'Get off, I don't need any help.'

Uncle Ralph ignores him and tries to hook his elbows underneath Dad's armpits.

'Get off!'

'Just relax and I'll lift you out. I've watched *Holby*, I know how to do it.'

'I don't need lifting, I can walk. You wouldn't be able to lift me anyway, you skinny little sod!'

'Stop making a fuss!'

Dad pushes Uncle Ralph's arms away. 'Just get out of the fucking way and let me get out.'

Afraid there's going to be a fight I put my arm on Uncle Ralph's shoulder and pull him away from the car.

'Just let Dad get out on his own.'

Uncle Ralph stands still but doesn't take his eyes off Dad and I realise he's just as scared as me.

Dad pulls himself gingerly out of the car and straightens up and draws a shaky breath.

'Get in then.'

'I'm walking.'

'Please Dad,' I say. 'Just get in. For me.'

Dad knows when he's beaten and he slowly lowers himself into the wheelchair with a sigh. As soon as his feet are on the foot plate Uncle Ralph whisks him away and Auntie Bridget and I have to trot to keep up with them. We reach the entrance and Auntie Bridget and I run in front of them to open the doors. Uncle Ralph manoeuvres the wheelchair through the doors and pushes the wheelchair straight up to the reception desk and parks Dad in front of it.

'My brother's having a heart attack,' he shouts at the receptionist. 'Call the crash team!'

The receptionist looks up at him slowly and doesn't even blink.

'Name?' she says, with a bored expression.

Uncle Ralph's mouth drops open and he looks at her in shock.

'Robert Sparkes,' I say.

'Occupation?'

'What does it matter what his bleeding job is?' Uncle Ralph leans over the counter and shouts at her. 'He's having a heart attack, you silly cow.'

Out of the corner of my eye I see a uniformed security guard straighten up from his slouched position of leaning against the wall. He rubs his hand over a stubbly chin and looks over at us with interest.

The receptionist looks at Ralph and without speaking points her pen at a laminated piece of paper tacked to the wall behind her.

No aggressive or threatening behaviour towards our staff will be tolerated.

Auntie Bridget kicks Uncle Ralph on the ankle.

Ralph clears his throat. 'Um. Yeah, Sorry about that.' Auntie Bridget prompts him with a glare. 'Please accept my sincere apologies.'

The receptionist looks slightly disappointed and out of the corner of my eye I see the security guard resume his slouched position against the wall.

'Occupation?' The pen is poised over the paper again.

'Accountant,' I say. She scribbles it down. 'He has chest pains. They're bad.'

'Wait here.' She slowly gets up from her seat and disappears through a doorway at the back of the office.

I bend down and look at Dad. 'You okay Dad?' *Please don't die, please don't die.*

Dad nods but doesn't speak.

A grey-haired nurse appears from the doorway at the back of the office and marches purposefully towards us.

She lifts up the counter flap and comes around and stands by Dad.
'Now, Mr Sparkes, we're going to take you through and see what's going on.' She pats him reassuringly on the shoulder. 'You'll be fine, don't worry.' She turns her attention to us. 'Now, who's next of kin?'

'Me.' Uncle Ralph and I both shout in unison.

She casts her eyes over us before she speaks. 'Okay. It's only supposed to be one of you but if you can keep out of the way you can all come with him.' She smiles and the three of us nod and follow her as she wheels Dad through two massive, automatic doors.

We enter a huge white room with rows of curtained cubicles, the nurse pushes Dad into the only empty one and helps him out of the wheelchair and onto the bed. With a tight smile to us she pulls a flowery curtain along in front of us.

'Just wait there please.' She says as she shuts herself behind the curtain and closes it with a firm tug.

The three of us stand awkwardly outside and look at each other, there are no seats and none of us know what to do. People dressed in green scrubs scuttle purposefully in and out of the rows of curtained cubicles that stretch down the room.

'Scrubs, that's what they're called,' says Uncle Ralph. 'Those green things, scrubs. They wear them for doing operations.'

'Do you think they'll have to operate on Dad?' I ask with horror.

'No, no of course not, pet.' Auntie Bridget glares at Uncle Ralph, 'Course they won't.'

The flowery curtain is opened with a swish and the grey-haired nurse pulls it back against the walls with a flourish.

'You can come in now.' She slots the clipboard onto the end of Dad's bed. 'Doctor will be along shortly.' She picks up a kidney shaped bowl from the cabinet and clips clops off in her efficient way.

Dad is sitting up in bed and is wearing just his trousers and socks and what looks like sticking plasters stuck all over his chest, with long wires attached to them that stretch to a complicated machine next to the bed. He looks a bit better now, not so grey and he's not sweating so much either. I feel relieved; he's in the right place, they'll look after him and make him better.

'ECG.' Dad points at the wires. 'Doing a heart trace. She took a load of blood too. Three bottles of it.' He shows us the plaster in the crook of his elbow.

The three of us crowd around the bed and intently watch the machine. None of us have a clue what the beeps mean.

We wait and watch the staff scurrying around. Uncle Ralph produces a packet of wine gums from his pocket and offers them around.

'Don't give Robbie one, you idiot,' says Auntie Bridget. 'What if he does need surgery? He can't eat anything.' She claps her hand over her mouth as soon as she's said it when she sees the horrified look on my face.

Oh God. Please let Dad be alright.

Uncle Ralph pops a wine gum in his mouth and wanders off in search of some chairs but finds only two. Auntie Bridget and I sit on them while Uncle Ralph perches on the end of the bed.

'How much longer?' Uncle Ralph asks. He seems a lot more relaxed now.

'For God's sake Ralph, can't you see they're busy? Now just shut your gob and be quiet,' Auntie Bridget hisses.

Uncle Ralph shrugs and shoves another wine gum in his mouth.

An hour and a half later one of the green scrubbed people appears. He has a stethoscope dangling around his neck so I'm guessing that he's the doctor. Uncle Ralph hurriedly jumps off the bed.

'Mr Sparkes? I'm Doctor Haskins. I understand you've been having chest pains?' He doesn't look at Dad but presses lots of buttons on the ECG machine and studies the changing numbers with a frown.

'Yes,' says Dad. 'They started about seven o'clock and got worse and worse.'

OMG. What if dad had died before I got home? I can't bear thinking about it.

'Hmm.' Doctor Haskins taps Dad's chest. 'And how is the pain now? Is it painful here or here?' He taps Dad's chest and before Dad can answer he puts the ends of the stethoscope in his ears, and lays the flat end of it on Dad's chest. He moves it around then gets Dad to lean forward and does the same on his back, frowning with concentration the whole time.

'Had any pains like this before?'

'A couple of times, but never this bad.'

He never told me! I feel a flash of anger; yet another secret he's kept from me.

'Is it my heart, doctor?' Dad asks in a shaky voice.

Doctor Haskins doesn't answer but takes the earpieces out of his ears and puts them back around his neck. 'A nurse will be along shortly and the blood tests should be back in about an hour. I'll come back then to discuss the results.'

Before any of us can say anything, the doctor disappears into the next cubicle and a different nurse materialises with a large beaker in her hand which she hands to Dad.

'Drink it straight down, please.'

'All of it? There's a lot there.'

'Please.'

Dad pulls a face; grey and milky looking, there's at least a pint of whatever it is.

We all watch as Dad gulps it down and the nurse whips the empty beaker off him and marches off.

'Wonder what that's for,' says Uncle Ralph.

'Could be they're going to do a scan or something,' Auntie Bridget answers.

Dad looks worried. 'I wish they'd just tell me what's going on.'

'You're in the best place, Dad. Nothing bad's going to happen to you here.' I say it with a confidence I don't feel.

We wait. Dad Dozes. Uncle Ralph keeps looking at his watch.

'What's the time?' Auntie Bridget asks for what seems like the twentieth time.

'Half past two.'

'Good job we'd haven't got work tomorrow.' Auntie Bridget yawns loudly.

'*We* have, haven't we Josie?'

I nod and Auntie Bridget looks at Uncle Ralph in annoyance.

'What! You don't have to go in, you own the place, remember?'

Uncle Ralph grunts.

In spite of my anxiety over Dad I can feel my eyes starting to close. Could I lie down next to Dad? Would anyone notice? Uncle Ralph could have my chair then. Too late; Uncle Ralph settles down onto the end of the bed and makes himself comfortable.

Dad drifts off to sleep and conversation comes to an end as we all nod off.

'Mr Sparkes?' Doctor Haskins is back.

Dad wakes with a snort and we all sit up, instantly awake. Uncle Ralph quietly slides off the bed.

Dad looks at Doctor Haskins expectantly.

'We have your results, Mr Sparkes.' He has a sheet of paper in his hand.

Chapter 19

Josie

It's still dark as we leave the hospital. And cold. I sit huddled in the back seat of the car and shove my hands underneath my armpits to keep them warm.

Uncle Ralph is not happy; it didn't help that when we came out of A&E there was a parking ticket on his car.

'For fuck's sake,' he said loudly, ripping the ticket off the windscreen. 'A parking ticket? A PARKING TICKET? What sort of traffic warden works through the night?' He screwed it up in a ball and threw it on the floor and kicked it and then marched around to the driver's side of the car and got in.

Auntie Bridget tried to shush him, but only half-heartedly. I think she'd had enough by then. I ran over and picked the ticket up, smoothed it out and put it in my pocket. Dad will probably pay it.

We race along the empty roads in silence, the only sound the roar of the heater on full blast. Eventually Uncle Ralph breaks the silence.

'I'll text Louise and tell her we won't be in today.'

'Okay,' I say.

'I was very impressed with the staff at the hospital,

very nice, I thought.' Auntie Bridget looks around from the front passenger seat and smiles. This is met with a snort from Uncle Ralph.

'Yeah, apart from that cow on reception. Got a good mind to put a complaint in about her.'

Auntie Bridget looks back at me and smiles and winks. 'Apart from her, I meant.'

'And the traffic warden,' Uncle Ralph barks. He's not happy.

'Look,' says Dad from the seat next to me. 'I'm really sorry you've all had a wasted night but there's nothing I can do about it.'

'Don't be silly,' says Auntie Bridget. 'You weren't to know and nor were we. You're okay and that's the main thing isn't it, Ralph?'

Uncle Ralph doesn't say anything and changes gear brutally as we turn into our street.

'Ralph?' Dad puts his hand on Uncle Ralph's shoulder.

We pull up in front of our house and come to an abrupt halt as Uncle Ralph slams on the brakes while simultaneously yanking the handbrake on.

'No, it's not your fault, mate, course it ain't.' Uncle Ralph turns the engine off and rubs his eyes. 'But I thought you were going to fucking die. Next time you have a hot curry, mate, take some Rennies, have a shit and save us all the worry.'

'Toast?' Dad asks.

'Please.' I sit down wearily at the table and watch as Dad fills the kettle and drops bread into the toaster. Skipper appears from the lounge and stands blinking at us from the kitchen doorway. When he's satisfied it's us, he makes a bee line for the back door and Dad opens it and lets him out.

'He must be bursting,' I say.

'Poor little sod. Bet he wondered what the hell was going on.'

'He probably slept most of the time.'

'Yeah.' Dad shakes his head in disbelief. 'God knows what that doctor at the hospital thinks of me. There's me thinking I was having a heart attack and it's indigestion, talk about embarrassing.'

'He did say it was an easy mistake, Dad, and that you weren't the first one to make that mistake and you won't be the last.'

'Yeah.' He digs his knife into the butter dish, loads it up and slaps a knife full onto the hot toast. 'But it doesn't stop me feeling like a complete idiot.'

He brings my toast over to the table and I tuck in; OMG a slice of toast never tasted so good.

'Well,' I say between mouthfuls, 'At least you know your heart's okay after all of the tests.'

'Yeah, there is that,' he says ruefully. 'Although I'll never hear the end of it from Ralph.'

No, he won't, not for years. 'He was so worried Dad, and so was I. We were frightened we were going to lose you.' I was so frightened, although I tried to hide it but there's no fooling Dad. He comes over and puts his arm around me.

'I'm not going anywhere, sweetheart, don't you worry. If anything, this has been a wakeup call for me.' He straightens up and pats his stomach. 'Time to start taking care of myself and stop being such a pig; get a bit of weight off.'

'You're not fat, Dad.'

'No, but I've got a bit of a pot belly coming, too much comfort eating.' He opens the door and lets

Skipper back in. 'Cut the portion sizes down, that's what I need to do.'

I smile. It won't last; he says this at least once a week.

'More toast?'

'No, I'm good. I'll pour the tea out.'

'I might have a couple more slices, because I'll probably sleep through lunch.'

See? Said it wouldn't last.

I pour the tea out and carry our mugs over to the table and sit down opposite him.

My eyes are heavy and I'm looking forward to crawling into bed for a few hours. But I won't be able to sleep until I know.

'So. About last night?'

Dad looks at me, eyebrows raised, cheeks bulging with hot buttered toast.

'Was Mum having an affair?'

Dad shakes his head. 'No! Of course not.'

'There's no point in lying Dad, I heard you talking, you might as well tell me.' Besides, I already know and the sad thing is that I thought *I* was protecting *you*.

I wait while he swallows his toast and washes it down with a mouthful of tea.

'I'm not lying.' He puts the cup down. 'Of course she wasn't having an affair, whatever gives you that idea?'

Do I tell him about the card and phone calls? What if he doesn't know? I decide to wait and see what he says.

'It sounded like she was from what I overheard, you said *he* nearly destroyed us.'

Dad looks at me thoughtfully.

'You might as well tell me because I'm not going to

be fobbed off and despite what you think, I'm not a child.'

'Okay. The reason we didn't tell you was because we didn't want to worry you.'

'Go on.'

'Your mother was being stalked.'

'Stalked?' I'm stunned.

'Yes. Stalked. She'd been getting some weird phone calls. Some weirdo would ring her and say he'd been watching her, had some fantasy that they were having a relationship, that they were going to be together. He said she was sending him messages.'

'Messages?'

'Yeah. Things like when she drew the curtains that meant she loved him, said it was their secret code. If she wore a certain colour to work that meant something else, weird shit like that.'

'He was clever though; if I picked the phone up, he'd put it straight down. I tried answering it and not speaking but somehow he guessed and I never managed to catch him out.'

The silent phone calls; he would only speak to her.

'Why didn't you go to the police?'

'We did. They said Mum had to keep a diary of everything that happened; suggested we change our phone number to stop the phone calls. We didn't want to do that, he would have won then, wouldn't he? But we were considering it. He was clever though; always withheld his number.'

'Didn't you have any idea who it was, at all?'

'No. And we tried, went through every person we knew, I knew, your mum knew. Friends, work colleagues, postman, you name it, we suspected them.'

'Surely the police could do *something*?'

Dad shakes his head. 'Told Mum to keep a diary, record the phone calls, be more self-aware, look at the people around her, you know, notice if she kept seeing the same person, that sort of thing. If we'd *known* who it was, they could have done something but apart from catching him red handed there wasn't a thing they could do.'

I was so convinced that Mum was having an affair. Poor Mum. I feel so bad for doubting her, for being so quick to think badly of her. I think back to her birthday; how I pretended to be ill when we came home from Rojanos because I thought she was cheating on Dad. I *avoided* her the next day. I feel sick. I could cry.

'Josie?' Dad is looking at me, concern etched onto his face. 'Are you okay sweetheart?'

I pull myself together. 'Yes, I'm just shocked.' A horrible thought strikes me. 'Did he threaten her?'

'No.' Dad shakes his head emphatically. 'Not at all. Just seemed to have this idea that they were having a relationship, that she was in love with him and they were going to be together. It spooked us a bit, about the secret code, because that meant that he was watching her sometimes and he obviously knew her because he knew where she lived and worked, so it could have someone she knew, or had met. Stupid really.' He laughs bitterly. 'But I started drawing the curtains after he said that, used to drop Mum at work when I could. Thing is, when I think back over those three months before she died, they're spoiled by *him*, by someone who had nothing to do with our lives but had an effect on it. Blighted it.'

He picks his cup up and drains the remaining tea.

'The only consolation I have is that Mum's last weekend with us was lovely, do you remember? We went to Rojano's, it was always Mum's favourite. It least he didn't spoil *that*.'

But he did, at least for Mum. I remember her face when she opened that card; what I took for guilt was fear. I know Mum and I know why she ripped it up and hid it in the bin; she didn't want it to spoil her birthday, spoil *our* day. So she hid it and pretended everything was fine so that we could enjoy it.

'I was surprised though, I was sure he would send flowers or something because he seemed to know a lot about Mum and I didn't think he'd let her birthday just go by. I felt better in a way because he couldn't have known everything about her. And typically, the postman decided to come early that day. I remember I came downstairs after I got dressed and the post had already come. I went flying back upstairs and burst into our bedroom and Mum took one look at my face and laughed and said *stop worrying nothing's going to spoil today*. I was so relieved. Especially when it turned out to be the last birthday she had with us. At least he didn't spoil that.'

I reach my hand across the table and hold Dad's hand and he gives me a sad smile.

I not going to tell him about the card now; there's absolutely no point and it'll ruin his memories of Mum's last day. I think that's a secret that I *should* keep.

'Come on.' He gets up and pushes his chair back. 'We need to get some sleep.'

'We do.'

'But I'm setting the alarm so we don't sleep all day, otherwise we'll be awake tonight.'

'Night, Dad.'

'Night, sweetheart.'

I have my foot on the bottom step of the stairs

when Dad grabs hold of me in a bear hug and holds me tight. We stand clinging onto each other for several minutes before he gently lets me go and I trudge up the stairs to bed.

I'm so tired I don't even bother to brush my teeth; I get undressed and put on my pyjamas and collapse into bed. I feel exhausted but will I be able to sleep? My mind is whirling around like a washing machine. I feel so happy that Mum *wasn't* having an affair and I got it so totally wrong. But I'm also angry at myself that I even thought she was capable. I shouldn't have been so disloyal; I should have known that Mum would *never* betray us. I offer up a silent prayer; *if you can hear me Mum, please forgive me. I am so, so sorry.*

Chapter 20

Robbie

So that's it, it's all out in the open now and Josie knows everything. Although I was against telling Josie about *him,* I had no choice when she caught me talking to Ralph. She's not a kid anymore and really, she had a right to know; it wasn't fair of me, Ralph and Bridget to keep it from her.

I suppose, thinking about it, that it must have sounded like Nessa was having an affair from what Josie overheard. Although I was a bit shocked that she could even *think* that about her Mum because that's something that Nessa would never, ever, do. She simply wasn't capable of being that devious or dishonest.

Nessa and I decided we wouldn't tell Josie about it when it was all happening because we didn't want to frighten and worry her. I know Josie would have been fretting every time Nessa left the house and we didn't want to make her as paranoid as we were. And I think we were right to keep it from her then; it wouldn't have done any good her knowing.

I'm still so angry about *him,* though. I'd like to get my hands on him and make him pay for the worry and upset he caused. I've even fantasised about finding out who he is and what I'd do to him to make him suffer, but realistically, we'll probably never find out who he is now. It's hardly going to be a priority for the police now, is it?

The good thing is that Josie seems so much better lately, more like her old self. It's amazing how much the counselling has helped, I didn't think after four weeks there'd be such a change. I encouraged her to go because I was desperate for some help for her but to be honest, I didn't see how just talking could make much difference.

Maybe *I* should have some counselling; talk to someone. I'm alright – and better than I was but it never goes away; the gut-wrenching loss. Time's supposed to be a great healer, and it is, but I almost feel guilty for wanting to get over losing Nessa. When she first died it was horrific; it was as much as I could do to drag myself out of bed every day. Although, when I woke in the morning, for those first few moments, I'd forget that she was gone and life seemed normal for a few seconds before I remembered and then it was like losing her all over again.

And the dreams; I used to dream about her every night, but I could never remember anything about them, only that she was in them. I used to think stupid things – like if I could time travel, I could go back and change things or travel to the future when it wouldn't hurt so much. For a few days I was convinced it was all a tragic mistake and Nessa would turn up and tell me it was all a terrible mix up.

Strange, the way your mind works.

But the most important thing is that Josie's getting back to the way she used to be before Nessa died. She's getting her confidence back and is so much happier and

I don't want to spoil that.

Which is the reason why I didn't tell her about the other thing that's bothering me; *he* must have known Nessa had died because he's not rung the house since. No more silent phone calls. Was he watching her when she went to London that day? Has he been watching me and Josie? Were we being watched at the funeral? Was he *there* at the church? There were so many people at the funeral, work colleagues of Nessa's, faces that I couldn't remember. *He* could have been there. Now Nessa's not here *he's* got no reason to watch the house but I can't stand not knowing who he is. Is it someone who knows us – is that how he knows Nessa's dead? Is it one of our friends?

I could drive myself mad with these thoughts and I have to make a conscious effort to stop myself, otherwise I'll end up in the nuthouse.

Look to the future, that's what we have to do. The past is done.

I could definitely have done without the humiliating trip to the hospital. Christ, I was mortified. I really thought I was having a heart attack and it was only indigestion! Unbelievable. I'm no wimp but there's no way I'd have believed indigestion could hurt so much; heartburn is a good description. The thing that terrified me the most was what would happen to Josie if I died? I know that Ralph and Brenda would take her in, course they would, they love her to bits. But I don't know if Josie could cope with losing me as well, not so soon after losing her mum.

So of course it was a massive relief when the doc said it was indigestion – and he was very nice about it. Said it was quite a common mistake and not to feel bad about it, better be safe than sorry and all that. But I did feel a right dick.

If Nessa was here, she'd have laughed until she cried.

Except of course it wouldn't have happened if she was still here because she wouldn't let me eat so much and make such a pig of myself. I need to *make an effort* as she was fond of saying so I'd better lay off the pies and start doing a bit of exercise. For Josie's sake as much as mine.

Ralph's never going to let me hear the end of it either, he'll be banging on about it for the next ten years. Although I caught the look on his face when he came and picked me and Josie up; I think he thought I was going to die.

All in all, it's been quite a day.

Chapter 21

Josie

Things are going right, so right. Amazingly I'm even enjoying going to college. Yes! Really, I feel like a new person or maybe the old version of me before Mum died.

I still miss Mum dreadfully but I feel I can miss her now without that awful guilt hanging over me about *keeping her secret* which turns out not to be true at all.

I'm my own worst enemy; I get on my own nerves. I should have done what most seventeen-year-olds would have done and told someone about it and then the last year of gradually feeling worse and worse could have been avoided. I'd have passed my exams and wouldn't have hit rock bottom and it would have been easier for Dad too. No, I have to make a complete drama out of it and imagine myself as some noble daughter guarding her mother's memory.

See, I am weird, what other seventeen-year-old would do that?

Although if I hadn't been a complete weirdo, I wouldn't have met Adam.

Which, I think, means that there's a reason why everything happens the way it does. I feel *so* bad about thinking Mum was a cheat when she was being stalked and I have to forgive myself for that. Because I wasn't in my right mind, I was grieving. Still am.

I just wish that Mum and Dad didn't have the stalking to spoil their last few months but I can't do anything about that so there's no point in worrying about the things that can't be changed, this is what Adam always tells me and he's right.

He's late today, or maybe I'm early. I don't know. I'm bursting to tell him about Mum and the stalking because I don't like him thinking badly of her. He probably hasn't given it a second thought, but I need to put the record straight.

I keep looking at my watch and he *is* late; a good ten minutes. I feel a bit annoyed, that's ten minutes of my time gone and I only get thirty minutes. We never run over the thirty minutes even if he's late arriving, he says it just puts all the appointments back if we run over. I don't think it's fair that Adam has to go to lots of different rooms for different appointments. Why can't he just see all of his clients in here? He says it's a matter of client confidentiality, that by going to a different room for each client none of us being counselled ever see each other. We're not all sitting in a waiting room looking at each other wondering what the others are here for, would be pretty awks if you think about it.

I suppose it makes sense; I don't care who knows I'm having counselling now but I did when I first started coming. I didn't want people to know and the thought of sitting in a waiting room with other people would have been horrific. Urgh.

He must have some really needy clients, although obviously he never tells me. Whenever he's late it because someone else has overrun and I always feel a little bit jealous because our sessions always end on time.

'Sorry!'

Adam comes crashing through the doorway looking flustered and my annoyance disappears. I'm just so pleased to see him.

He bangs the door shut and sits down opposite me, out of breath.

'Sorry,' he says again. 'Bit of a situation, nearly never got here at all.'

'That's okay.'

'I'm really sorry.' He looks at his watch. 'Because it's cut our time down quite a bit.' He flips his note book open. 'Or maybe the next client will have to wait.' He gives me a lovely smile.

I feel a fizz of happiness; he's never said that before.

'So, you look glowing, what's been happening?'

I feel my face redden, I can't help it. The slightest hint of a compliment from Adam and it happens.

'I found out that Mum wasn't having an affair at all!' I almost shout at him.

'Say that again I didn't quite catch it.' Adam is looking at me with a confused expression on his face.

I was in such a hurry to tell him that it came out in a rush and he probably has no idea what I'm talking about so I take a deep breath and say it again, more slowly.

Adam nods his head thoughtfully. 'And how do you know this?' he asks seriously.

I feel disappointed; why isn't he as thrilled as I am? But of course he's not, why would he be? *And* I haven't even told him what's happened over the weekend.

'When I got home from band practice on Friday night Dad was talking to my Uncle Ralph on the phone and I overheard him. I wasn't eavesdropping or anything, I just happened to hear. Then Dad had a heart attack, but he didn't really, so we had to take him to hospital...'

'Whoa! You've lost me. Your Dad had a heart attack?'

'No. It was indigestion,' I say impatiently. 'But we thought it was a heart attack so we spent the night in A&E and when we got home...'

'Josie?' Adam interrupts and I look at him. 'You're babbling. I've never seen you babble before but I like it. But you need to slow down a bit because I can't keep up.'

I blush again at the slightest hint of a compliment.

I take a deep breath and start again. 'So. Dad thought he was having a heart attack but it turned out to be indigestion from a very hot curry.'

I see the hint of a smile from Adam which he tries to hide.

'I know.' I laugh. 'He's beyond embarrassed. Anyway, we got home from the hospital and I made him tell me what he was talking about in the phone call to Uncle Ralph. I asked him if Mum was having an affair.'

Adam leans forward. 'What did he say?'

'He said of course she wasn't and whatever had given me that idea?'

'And what did you say?'

'I said it sounded like it from what he'd said. I didn't tell him about the birthday card.'

'Go on.'

'He said that Mum was being stalked.' Saying it makes me feel sad, for Mum, for Dad. It must have been *so* horrible for them.

Adam is stunned. 'Stalked?'

'Yeah. Stalked. Some weirdo had been ringing her; he thought he was in a relationship with her. Dad said he'd been watching her and stuff. A mental case. I don't really want to waste my breath talking about *him*; the main thing is that Mum wasn't having an affair.'

'That must have been a shock.'

'It was, poor Mum and Dad, they must have been so worried.'

'You're sure this is what really happened? You don't think your Mum was really having an affair and your Dad didn't want to tell you?'

I look at Adam in shock. This wasn't the reaction I'd been expecting; I thought he'd be as delighted as me. And I *know* that Dad would never lie to me.

'No. Definitely not. The police had got involved and they would have caught him if Mum hadn't died, it was only a matter of time.'

'Sorry Josie, I'm just playing devil's advocate here, I just need to be sure you've thought this all through.'

'Okay.' I can't help feeling a bit deflated though.

'You must feel relieved.'

'I do, massively. But I also feel really bad for thinking the worst of Mum.'

'There's no point....'

'...in worrying about things you can't change.' I join in and we say it together.

We both laugh. 'You know me too well,' Adam says. His notebook slips off his knee onto the floor and we look at it on the floor then both lean down to pick it up at the same time.

I reach it first and as I straighten up to hand it to Adam, he's looking straight at me. Our eyes lock and he slowly places his hand on top of my hand and holds it

177

tight.

For a moment I can't breathe; he's so close to me I can smell his aftershave and feel his breath on my cheek. We stare into each other's eyes and I can't move. The air feels charged, like the moment before a thunderstorm. Adam leans towards me and our lips touch briefly before he lets go of my hand and slowly sits back.

The spell is broken and I gaze at Adam in wonder; he kissed me, he *must* feel the same way about me as I do about him.

He clears his throat. 'I'm so sorry. I should never have done that.'

'Don't say sorry, don't tell me that you didn't mean it.' My voice sounds small and shaky. I can't bear it if he tells me it was a mistake and meant nothing to him. I hand the notebook over and continue to stare at him, willing him to say he feels the same.

'I did mean it.' He smiles. 'And you wouldn't believe how long I've wanted to do that, but...'

'But what?'

'It's not appropriate, I can't be your counsellor and have a relationship with you.'

'I'll get another counsellor.'

Adam smiles sadly. 'Actually, I don't think you need one anymore, but that's not the point. I can't have a relationship with someone I've counselled. And you're underage.'

'I'm not! I'm seventeen.'

'You're under eighteen. That's underage.'

'We could keep it a secret,' I say.

'No.' Adam shakes his head but I think maybe I could persuade him, he doesn't look completely sure.

'I'll be eighteen this year, then I can do what I like.'

'I'm a lot older than you, I'm twenty-nine.'

'Only eleven years. That's nothing. Lots of people have older partners.' Did I really say *partner*? Adam doesn't laugh at me but sits staring at his notebook.

'I'll get the sack if anyone finds out that I kissed you; I'd probably be banned from counselling anyone ever again.' He looks so worried.

I'd *never* tell anyone.

'I won't tell a soul,' I say.

'But what if it came out, chatting to Biro or Ellie, you might say something without realising and that'd be the end of me. I'd be unemployable.'

I lean forward and reach out for his hand. He has long, slim, fingers; *pianist's fingers,* Mum would call them, with neat, square nails. I hold his hand in both of mine, enjoying the feeling of touching him, touching his skin.

'You don't have to worry. At all. I'm good at keeping secrets, remember?'

Free. That's how I feel. Liberated, and happy. So, so happy. The rest of today passed in a blur because I couldn't really take anything in after my counselling with Adam. I kept thinking about what had happened, our kiss, and it was just amazing. I wish it could have gone on forever. He's *so* gorgeous. And he wants me! Me! Adam feels the same about me as I feel about him, I can't believe it!

Yes, I know it's not appropriate but like Adam says, nothing can happen while he's still my counsellor but a few more weeks and he won't be. Obviously, I won't be able to tell anyone for quite a while but I can keep a secret, I kept Mum's, or so I thought. This is different though, this is a nice secret, a lovely secret that I can hug to myself and enjoy.

I'll have to be a bit careful because people *have* noticed a change in me and I don't want to get Adam into trouble. Biro kept asking me what I was so cheerful about and I noticed him giving me that sideways appraising look that he does when he's thinking so I'll have to contain it a bit, try to act normal.

Dad noticed too; we were eating dinner and he said how much I've changed and I said well the counselling's working Dad and he was so pleased. Said he'd maybe get Uncle Ralph some, it might stop him being such a misery.

But now I'm in bed and there's only me and Skipper here so I can lie here and remember what happened today and it won't matter if I've got a silly smile on my face or a dreamy look in my eyes.

He's so gorgeous. And he wants me! I can't believe it.

What a day! I can't wait until Friday to see him again. Yes, I know we can only talk and nothing inappropriate can happen but surely a little kiss wouldn't hurt? And a hug maybe? I'm suddenly grateful that the counselling room is so out of the way; I don't want Adam to lose his job or his career because of me. I'd never forgive myself.

Skipper creeps up from the bottom of the bed and snuggles up next to me and gives a big sigh. I wrap my arms around him and gaze into his furry little face.

'I'm in love, Skipper,' I whisper, because I want to say it, I want to share it. Skipper gazes at me and blinks.

I'm *so* happy.

Chapter 22

Josie

'Whassup with you?' Biro says through a mouthful of bacon baguette.

I look at him in surprise. 'Nothing, why?'

'You seem different, that's all.'

'Just the same as I've always been.' I take a bite of my cheese sandwich and try not to blush.

'You seem happier,' says Ellie. 'More your old self.'

'My old self when?' I ask.

Ellie colours and realises what she's said.

'It's okay, Ellie. I know I was a nightmare when Mum died but I think I'm getting back to normal now.' Or a new version of normal, anyway.

She smiles, relieved that I haven't taken offence.

'I suppose.' Biro shoves the rest of the baguette into his mouth. 'We've got the wonderful Adam to thank for that.'

I frown and ignore him and carry on eating my sandwich. Whenever he refers to Adam now, he calls him *the wonderful Adam* and he doesn't even attempt to hide his dislike. I've stopped talking about him but the less I talk about him the more Biro brings him into the conversation. I've talked to Ellie about it and she said perhaps he's jealous of Adam. I couldn't stop laughing when she said that.

'Ellie,' I said. 'Don't you realise that Biro fancies *you*?'

She said, 'No, of course he doesn't.' But I could tell she was pleased. I told her I thought they'd make a lovely couple and I was sure anytime soon Biro would be asking her out.

Biro scrunches the paper wrapper up into a ball and wipes his mouth with it and then drinks about half a bottle of coke in one swallow.

'Did you ask him about his mum then?'

'What?'

'Did you ask the wonderful Adam why he said his mum was dead?'

'Of course I didn't, you've obviously got it wrong.'

'No, I haven't.'

'You're not always right, Biro. You can get things wrong sometimes you know.'

'Ask him then, prove me wrong.'

'I don't need to ask him and anyway, it'd sound a bit odd wouldn't it? Are *you sure your mum's dead cos my mate says she isn't.* And why would he even lie? What would be the point of that? I don't know why you're making such a big deal out of it.'

Biro shrugs. 'Dunno. Don't trust him is all. He's shady.'

'Shady? How can you say that? You don't even know him!'

Biro noisily draws air in through his nose and narrows his eyes and looks at me.

'Just a feeling I've got. Definitely shady.'

'You've never actually met him.'

'Don't need to. Even his family don't like him.'

I laugh, and hope it doesn't sound as false as it feels. 'What *are* you talking about?'

'Parents chucked him out, y'know, his father and *dead* mother. Bit of a secret why but they defo chucked him out. He didn't go far though, lives in the next street, next to the paper shop.'

'And?' I'm getting fed up with this, why is he so obsessed with Adam?

'Probably thought it was about time he left, bit sad living at home at his age,' Ellie chips in, and I glare at her.

'Just saying,' she says and looks down. 'They probably thought it was about time he got his own place.'

'Nope. They defo chucked him out,' Biro says emphatically.

'Oh, shut up Biro, you're being ridiculous.'

'Just looking out for a mate, that's all.'

OMG. He's so infuriating, there's no reasoning with him.

'You don't need to look out for me, he's my counsellor, that's all. Anyway, I've only got a few more sessions and that's me done.'

'Yeah, give it a rest, Biro,' Ellie says. 'It's not like Josie's going to fancy him or anything, he's *old*.'

He's not that old, I want to say, he's only twenty-nine, but obviously I don't.

'Yeah,' I say, rolling my eyes. 'As if.'

Two more nights until I see Adam. I feel like a kid counting sleeps before Christmas. I'm not exactly counting the hours but I can't wait; it seems like forever. Every time I'm in the cafeteria I look for him but I haven't seen him this week. I've seen the tutor that I thought was his girlfriend, she's really pretty, much prettier than I remembered. I feel so proud that he's chosen me over her and I keep thinking I should pinch myself to make sure it's not some lovely dream that I'm going to wake up from at any minute.

Biro is getting on my nerves but I'm not going to let him spoil it for me. He's my best friend and he always will be but I don't need him to tell me what to do or to look out for me. He's just being ridiculous about Adam and I don't know what's got into him. I'm sad in a way that Biro's being so awkward because I know that if he didn't have this thing about Adam, I could confide in him and he wouldn't tell a soul. I can trust Biro with anything. I'm bursting to share how Adam and I feel about each other with someone but I know that I daren't; Adam would lose his job and I'd never forgive myself so we'll just have to wait until I'm eighteen. I have been talking to Skipper though, because he's hardly going to tell anyone, is he?

I've felt a bit unsettled the last couple of days but I don't know why. At first I thought it was because of all of the excitement of kissing Adam and admitting our feelings to each other, but it's not that. I'm totally okay with how I feel about him, I wish I could shout it from the rooftops but I know I can't. I suppose I do feel a bit deceitful about keeping it secret, especially from Dad, but there's nothing I can do about it at the moment. Dad definitely wouldn't understand; about the age gap let alone it being inappropriate because of the counselling. But it's not as if we're doing anything wrong is it? I mean, we only talk, we won't start a relationship until the counselling has finished.

I don't know what it is that's bothering me but there's definitely something. I slept really well on

Tuesday night and woke feeling so happy apart from something niggling at the edge of my mind. Maybe it was a dream I'd had and then couldn't remember, something I couldn't grasp. Something's telling me that it's important but it's floating around just out of reach and just when I think I'm about to grasp it, it flits away.

It's very annoying because I just want to wallow in my feelings for Adam and enjoy them and then this maddening feeling keeps telling me I've missed or forgotten something important. I blame Biro; I wish he would just stop going on and on and spoiling everything. I don't want to have to choose between Biro and Adam.

Adam and I decided that we wouldn't text each other unless absolutely necessary. Obviously when my counselling has finished, we'll have to decide how we're going to see each other, then sort things out. When Biro told me where Adam lives, I was so pleased. I'll be able to go and see him and no one will know, we can keep our relationship a secret. I can get Dad to drop me off at Biro's and walk round to Adam's, Biro won't approve but I don't think he'd dob me in even though he doesn't like Adam.

I can't wait.

I awake with a start; it's still dark.

I was dreaming about Mum and her birthday and our last weekend together. I touch my face and wipe away the tears that I've been crying in my sleep.

The dream about Mum wasn't the reason I woke up and I wish I could go back to sleep and forget; forget what my brain has somehow remembered while I've been sleeping, forget what's been eating away at the back of my mind for days.

Maybe I'm wrong.

I wish I was wrong but I know that I'm not.

I turn the bedside light on; 4:30, there's no chance of going back to sleep now. I feel wide awake and I feel sick; sick at what I've remembered.

But it doesn't make any sense at all.

I lie there and stare at the ceiling, thoughts tumbling around in my head, round and round, like clothes in a tumble dryer.

Why?

I lie like this for what seems like hours, trying to make sense of it. Skipper senses I'm awake and crawls from the end of my bed to lie on my chest. It's uncomfortable and he feels like a lead weight but I wrap my arms around him and hold him tight.

Why?

I turn my head to look at the clock again, 5:37.

I lift Skipper off me and get out of bed, pad across the room and pick up my laptop from the desk. I get back into bed but I don't lie down. I prop the laptop on my lap and turn it on and wait for what seems like forever for it to boot up.

At last the screen flickers to life and I open Google.

I have some searching to do.

Chapter 23

Josie

I hide down the side of the shed between an old ladder and the garden fence. The shed slats are broken and split and keep snagging my Parka as I move. I wonder how long I'll have to wait for.

Thursday is dustbin day; or so the council website tells me. I've been here since eight o'clock; I told Dad I was going into college early for an extra exam revision class. He seemed so pleased that I was *keen* as he put it and I felt disgusted with myself for lying.

A lot of dustbins were already out in the street when I arrived and I thought then that I'd wasted my time and I'd got here too late so I might as well go home. But then I realised that they'd put them out last night, like Dad does, and that not everyone does that.

I sort of felt relieved for a minute when I thought I was too late, it would have been the perfect get out and I could forget this stupid idea and not do this.

But I had to be sure in my own mind so I walked up the alleyway at the back of the houses, counting them as I walked; checked that I had the right house and slipped in through the back gate, which luckily for me was open. Or unluckily. I closed the gate as quietly as I could and prayed that he wasn't looking out of the window; or that he chose that minute to come out of the back door. I could see the dustbin was still next to the back door, and wondered if he wouldn't bother putting it out at all and then I'll have wasted my time.

But I'm going to wait a bit longer, now I'm here. I shiver. I have my Parka on with the hood up but it's bitterly cold and damp and my feet are freezing. I want to stamp my feet and flap my arms around to keep warm but I daren't. I look at my watch again; I've only been here ten minutes but it feels like forever.

Am I mad? I think maybe I am going a little mad.

In the quietness I hear the sound of a door being opened and I slowly peer around the shed to see a figure coming out of the back door. He grabs the handle of the wheelie bin and trundles it towards me. I press myself back against the shed and hold my breath, not trusting myself to breathe quietly. I hear the squeak of the gate as it's opened and the sound of the bin being rolled through into the alley way.

He'll have to go along the alley and take it around to the front of the house so I have a few minutes now before he comes back. No one bothers to lock their door when they put the bin out, do they? What's the point when they'll only be a few minutes.

I force my feet to move and I come out from my hiding place, carefully holding the ladder so it doesn't clatter and then I sprint down the garden path and into the house. The back door opens straight into the kitchen and I dash inside and pause for a moment; I need to think quickly because I don't have long until he comes back. The kitchen is small and basic, a few base and wall cupboards, a washing machine, cooker and fridge; there's nowhere to hide in here.

I run through the door into a hallway, the front door is at the end and the lounge opens off it to the side. I look in the lounge for somewhere to hide; there's a large sofa in front of the bay window, a massive television on a chipped pine unit and a rickety table with four mismatched chairs around it.

Click.

The sound of the backdoor being opened.

A horrifying thought hits me; did I leave the back door in the same position as he left it? I have no idea and it's too late now.

I tiptoe over to the sofa and squeeze between the back of the sofa and the bay window and crouch down and hold my breath.

I hear the sound of the back door being closed and locked.

Silence, then the heavy thump of footsteps going up the stairs.

More silence.

I can hear him walking around upstairs and then the sound of footsteps coming down the stairs. I wonder if he's here in the lounge; I can't hear his footsteps because of the carpet. I clap my hand over my mouth, because I'm so scared I think I might start crying.

I feel almost dizzy with relief when I hear the sound of the front door being unlocked, opened, then closed and locked.

I wait and let my breath out slowly and silently.

I look at my watch and decide that I'll wait ten minutes to make sure he's gone before I move.

Ten minutes crawl by and I wait ten minutes more.

I'm too scared to move, almost paralysed with fear.

What if he comes back?

I can't stay here can I? I force myself to move and

immerge from my hiding place. If he comes back I'll hear him and have time to hide or get out, so stop being so dramatic, Sparkes.

I decide to start upstairs.

At the top of the stairs there are two bedrooms, one either side of the stairs. I go into the front one first which has a double bed, a battered chest of drawers and a rickety wooden dining chair. The wardrobe is basically an alcove with a striped curtain across instead of a door. I pull the curtain aside and search through his clothes. I'm careful to leave everything as I find it. Hangers full of trousers, shirts, shoes jumbled on the floor. All the normal things you'd expect to find in a wardrobe, nothing more. I have a moment of excitement when I spy an old shoe box tucked underneath the bed. I stretch my hand under the bed and pull it out and my heart is racing when I open it to reveal a pair of battered trainers. Well, what did I expect?

The second bedroom is full of junk; a couple of suitcases, an empty box from the television in the lounge; cardboard boxes with books, magazines, CDs and DVDs tossed in them. This house feels unlived in and unloved, it doesn't feel like a home, more just a place to sleep. It's cold, too.

I don't spend long in the bathroom; a horrible green bath, faded white in places with a green sink and toilet. I open the mirrored bathroom cabinet on the wall above the sink to find a razor, a toothbrush, toothpaste, deodorant. I close the door and my own reflection stares back at me; pale faced and hollow eyed from lack of sleep.

What am I doing? My reflection asks.

I come back along the landing and down the narrow, threadbare carpeted stairs. I can't get warm and I can't wait to get out of here and go home.

The kitchen is so small and basic that there's nowhere to hide anything. I open one cupboard to be confronted by cans: baked beans, spaghetti, soup, pies in a tin and half a white sliced loaf sitting on top of them. The cupboard next to it: four dinner plates, two cups and one bowl. I search the cupboard under the sink: a bottle of washing up liquid and an empty bottle of bleach.

The fridge holds a container of margarine, a slab of cheese and a pint of milk.

Nothing.

I feel depressed; not just at the lack of finding anything but at the state of the house. Who lives like this? I experience a moment of pity and then tell myself not to be so stupid.

I search the lounge and find nothing, what did I expect, seriously? I'm starting to feel a bit foolish now. Am I wrong? Have I got it all wrong? Have I made a terrible mistake? Have I misjudged him entirely?

No. I know I haven't.

I zip up my Parka and check the rooms to make sure I've left no trace of my visit. I'll slip out of the back door and no one will ever know that I've been here; *he'll* never know.

Except that I can't find the key to the back door, a solid, white plastic door that can't be opened without a key. I pull open the kitchen drawers one after the other; one holds cheap cutlery, the other, threadbare tea towels.

A frantic search of the kitchen reveals what I've already guessed; no key. Okay, I'll just have to go out of the front door and hope that a nosey neighbour isn't watching.

Which is when I discover that there's no key for the front door either.

I'm locked in.

There must be a window I can climb out of but I check the lounge and kitchen and they're all locked too. This is the shabbiest, most basic house imaginable but it has new plastic windows and doors that are impossible to open unless you have the key. I go back upstairs and check the bedrooms for a key but there's nothing. A small window in the bathroom is open which I could probably just about get through but without a ladder how would I get down? Why did I think this was such a great idea at half-past-five this morning?

I stand looking at the street through the grubby net curtains of the lounge window. I know I have no choice and I'll never hear the end of it, but I'll have to ring Biro. I look at my watch, 9:45. I just hope he hasn't left for college yet. I press the call button and he picks up on the third ring.

'Yo! You alright mate?'

'No. Where are you?'

'Eh? Just leaving for college, why?'

'I need your help.'

'What's happened?'

I quickly tell him where I am and how I'm locked in.

'You're WHERE?' he shouts at me in shock. 'WHY?'

'I'll explain later, just come now and help me get out. I can climb out of the bathroom window. There's a ladder down the side of the shed. Put it up to the window and I'll climb out.'

'Okay, be there in a minute. You've got some fucking explaining to do.'

Relief floods me 'Thanks, Biro, you're the best.'

'I'm at the end of the street. Be there in a couple of minutes.'

'Okay.' I'm about to hang up when I see a car pull up outside the house. I don't recognise the car but I know the person inside it. I don't understand why he's come back? I didn't think he'd be home for hours.

'Biro! He's back! He's outside the house!' I whisper into the phone.

'Fuck! Stay out of sight and hide.' He kills the call.

I drop down to the floor before he sees me through the window and crawl back into my hiding place behind the sofa. My heart is pounding, what am I going to do? I'm trapped.

I hear the sound of a key in the lock and the front door being opened and closed. And locked.

This is it; I can't get out now. Talk yourself out of this, Sparkes.

What am I going to do?

I hear the sound of him coming into the lounge when there's a sudden loud banging on the front door and non-stop ringing of the doorbell. The footsteps falter, then stop for a moment.

I hold my breath.

The banging gets even louder and the footsteps fade and go back out into the hallway and I hear the door being unlocked and yanked open.

'WHAT?'

'Hey, mate. I've just seen a couple of lads going into your back garden. Looked like they were up to no good.' It's Biro's voice. He's almost shouting.

'What? When was this?' He sounds annoyed.

'Just now. I'll come and have a look with you.' I hear Biro's voice get even louder and it sounds like he's pushed his way into the hallway.

'Hey. Hang on...'

I peek around the side of the sofa to see Biro clomping down the hall to the kitchen. 'Can't be too careful these days...' he shouts, and I hear the rattle of the back-door handle. 'If you open this, we could have a look.'

'Look, thanks for telling me but there's no need to barge into my house.' Adam's voice is coming from the kitchen too.

'Sorry mate,' Biro says loudly. 'We'll just have a look and I'll be off.'

I listen with my breath held and hear the rattle of a bunch of keys, he must be opening the back door. It's now or never.

I creep out from behind the sofa and tiptoe across the lounge to the doorway where I pause for a moment. I can see the front door is ajar and I make a run for it and slip into the hallway and out of the front door. I run down the street as fast as I can and I don't stop running until I'm three streets away. I stand doubled over with my hands on my knees gulping for air and trying to catch my breath.

I searched the house and found nothing and nearly missed what was right there in front of me the whole time.

The last Christmas present I gave Mum was a scarf; pink, shot through with blue swirls and Robins, her favourite bird, scattered all over. Mum had lots of scarves but that was her favourite and she wore it loads. After she died, we never saw that scarf again; Dad thought Mum was wearing it the day she died but he wasn't sure and he tortured himself about that too; the fact that he couldn't remember exactly what she was wearing that day. I told him; why should you remember? It was just a day like any other, we didn't *know* what was going to happen. We never got any of Mum's belongings back after her death; everything had been destroyed by the train so we never knew if she was wearing it or not.

But she couldn't have been wearing it.

Because as I ran out of Adam's house, I saw that scarf.

It was hanging on a peg in the hallway.

Chapter 24

Josie

I sit and wait at a table in Joey's Cafe, not far from the Rise, the local common, waiting for Biro to arrive. It's cheap, sort of cheerful and always smells of a mixture of fried eggs and coffee.

I take a sip of my hot chocolate but it tastes of nothing; I think my taste buds are in shock and not working. I trace the brown swirls on the table with my finger and try to process what's just happened. Biro texted to say he'd meet me here and I'm just starting to get worried that he's not coming when the door flies open and he comes in on a blast of cold air. He shoves the door shut with a bang and glances at me unsmilingly then walks past me to the counter. I hear him ordering his drink then he clomps over and sits down opposite me. The thought pops into my head that he never does anything quietly and I have to stifle a hysterical giggle.

'You okay?' I say.

'No. What,' he leans forward and lowers his voice, 'The fuck, were you doing in his house?'

I stare at him dumbly unable to think of anything I can say that would make any sort of sense.

'He's not stupid, when I knocked at the door, he knew I was up to something but he didn't know what, just kept saying he knew me, that I looked familiar. I said I just have one of those faces but I could tell he didn't believe me.' Biro is frowning so hard I think he's going to go cross eyed. 'He practically threw me out of the front door.'

I continue to stare then draw a shaky breath. 'You were right all along, Biro. You were right about him.'

We're interrupted by Joey putting Biro's cappuccino in front of him on the table. We wait until he's out of earshot.

'He's a weirdo,' says Biro quietly. 'I know that, but that doesn't explain what you were doing breaking into his house.'

'I didn't break in, I slipped in when he was putting his bin out and then I was locked in because you need a key to get out.'

'I don't know what you're talking about so tell me it all, from the beginning.'

'I never told you about my Mum being stalked, did I?' I say.

Biro looks shocked. 'Stalked? No.'

I tell him about the months of phone calls, the secret codes and the birthday card.

'What's this got to do with Adam?' I think he's guessed, he just wants me to confirm it.

'It's him. He dropped his notebook on the floor in my counselling session on Tuesday and I picked it up. I didn't realise straight away. When I saw his writing in the notebook, I knew it was him. It's the same writing as the birthday card that was sent to Mum.'

Biro looks at me in disbelief. 'And you broke into his house on the strength of a *birthday card*? You didn't think he might just have similar writing? You saw that card a long, long time ago. Once. I can't believe you broke into his house on the strength of some fucking handwriting that may or may not be his.'

Biro's voice is getting louder and Joey glances over at us with a frown.

'Mate, really?' Biro whispers. '*Really*?'

'I have an eidetic memory,' I say.

He looks at me blankly.

'Photographic. I have a photographic memory. I only need to see stuff once and I remember it.'

'Yeah,' he says, unconvinced. 'But he could just have the same writing, it's not proof is it? Fuck me, Josie, it hardly warrants a bit of breaking and entering, does it? What did you think you'd find? Photos of your mum plastered all over the walls or something?'

I don't know what I expected to find; all I know is that once I'd remembered, I was sure, absolutely certain. I had no proof at all and I've surprised myself with how certain I am, how ready I am to believe the worst of Adam.

When I thought the very best of him.

'No, it's not proof,' I say. 'And I was seriously doubting myself when I didn't find anything, starting to think that maybe I'd got it all wrong. But then I saw the scarf.'

Biro listens while I tell him about the scarf.

'Now do you believe me?' If he doesn't believe me, I have no hope that anyone else will. Am I going mad? Am I imagining things?

'Yeah I do believe you, but others might not.'

I feel a rush of relief.

'Because, er...' Biro hesitates, 'The fact that you're having counselling and have had problems could go against you.'

'I know.' I fight back tears. 'People will think I'm mental.'

'Which is why we need proof.'

'I know.' It's unlikely that anyone is going to believe me. *I* wouldn't believe me.

'So, how do we prove it?'

'I don't know. But that's not all of it.' I feel despondent and foolish.

Biro narrows his eyes and looks at me.

'I thought I was in love with Adam.'

'Go on.'

'And I thought he was in love with me.' I look down at the table as a tear rolls down my cheek and I brush it angrily away.

'But now I don't know what's going on. Why would he do that to me? Did he know who I was before the counselling? Did he *plan* it? Why? Why would he pretend to have feelings for me? I don't understand any of it.' I can't hold it back any longer and I start to sob. Biro silently hands me a paper napkin and I blow my nose and try to compose myself. 'I'm just a stupid idiot,' I snivel.

'No, you're not. He groomed you.'

'No he didn't. I'm not a kid.'

'Yes, he did,' Biro says angrily. 'He's supposed to be helping you and he used his position to take advantage of you.'

'Nothing's happened.'

Biro looks at me.

'Sexually, I mean.'

'Would have done though, wouldn't it? Bastard. Bloke's a sicko, like I always said. Something up with him. He needs to be stopped.'

'How? I can't exactly tell anyone that I've been in his house, can I?'

'You can at least report him for inappropriate behaviour, counsellors aren't supposed to behave like that.'

I don't know what to do. There's no proof, apart from Mum's scarf, and he could just say he found it in the street, it's hardly conclusive.

'You could ask him,' Biro says thoughtfully.

'What? Is that supposed to be funny? I never want to see him again.' I look at Biro in shock.

'Go to your counselling tomorrow and confront him, see what he has to say for himself.'

I shake my head. 'I can't, I don't think I can even talk to him. I definitely don't want to be alone with him.'

'You wouldn't be alone, I could hide somewhere and record it.' Biro holds his phone up. 'I can record it on here and if you feel frightened just shout out and I'll come out of hiding.'

'I don't know if I'm brave enough.'

'Course you are. And if *you're* not, *I'll* confront him.'

'Do you think it could work?' I ask tentatively.

'Mate,' Biro says confidently, warming to his idea, 'I know it will.'

'He'll probably deny everything,' I say.

'Yeah, well, if he does, we'll just have to leave it to the police but without a confession or proof he'll probably get away with it. At least this way we've got a chance of catching him out.'

'Okay, let's do it.'

'What have we got to lose,' says Biro. 'It's worth a try.'

'I suppose so.' Why do I feel as though I'm in some

skewed version of an Enid Blyton adventure?

'Right. I'll get us another drink and we'll work out a plan.'

Biro jumps up and goes up to the counter.

I can't wait for the next twenty-four hours to be over.

Chapter 25

Josie

I'm early. Sitting in my usual chair waiting for Adam to arrive.

Biro and I have been here for nearly half an hour; we came extra early, just in case Adam decided to get here first for a change.

My legs keep shaking and I have to keep my feet firmly planted on the ground to stop them or else Adam will notice. I feel sick too but Biro seems quite the opposite, so keyed up and excitable that I'm not sure how he's going to contain himself when he has to hide. I think he's enjoying himself and imagines he's in a TV programme.

Biro turns his head from the doorway where he's been hanging about for the last half-an-hour and puts his finger over his lips in a shushing motion.

'He's coming,' he mouths.

My stomach does a lazy flip and I try to swallow but my mouth is bone dry.

Biro steps back from the doorway and pads quietly to the corner of the room and squeezes himself into the narrow gap between a tall metal cupboard and the wall. Adam won't see him; or he won't unless he goes looking for him. Biro holds his phone up and winks as he disappears from sight.

'Hi! Sorry I'm late.' Adam breezes in and shuts the door then flings himself down into the chair opposite with a big smile.

'Hi,' I say, my own smile feels like a tight mask stretched across my face and my lips feel as if they're stuck to my teeth. It must be so obvious that I'm not the same as normal.

Adam looks the same - or does he? Perhaps because I'm seeing him from a different perspective, I find fault with him. Is that smile really sincere or is it fake? And why is he nearly *always* late? He hardly ever gets here on time. Or is that part of the grooming process – making me wait for him?

'So…' He puts his notebook on his lap, just as he usually does. 'How has your week been?' That smile again.

In an instant my nervousness vanishes and is replaced by a hatred so fierce that I don't know how I'm going to hold it in. All I can think about is what he did to Mum, how he spoiled her last few months with me and Dad. And for what he's tried to do to me, whatever that is – in his sick mind. Wasn't stalking Mum enough? Was making me fall in love with him some sort of revenge? Because I did imagine I was in love with him but it was just a stupid teenage crush because how can you love someone when you barely know them? I imagined I loved him based on twice weekly meetings of thirty minutes. What a stupid, immature idiot I am. I barely know him.

And I thought I was mature! I'm embarrassed for myself.

'Interesting,' I finally answer him with a voice I

barely recognise.

'Really?' He seems oblivious to my mood and my hatred for him ramps up a notch and I almost shout at him.

'Why did you never tell me that you knew who my mother was?'

If I expected him to look shocked, I'm disappointed; the smile never falters.

'Didn't ask, did you?' That smile again.

I look at him in confusion; this wasn't the reaction I was expecting. I don't know what to say next, this isn't going according to the plan.

'You don't think you should have told me?' I snap.

'Look.' He leans forward, elbows on his knees, closing the gap between us. 'You've obviously made up your mind about me or you wouldn't have broken into my house, would you?'

I sit as far back as my chair will allow. He's too close. He *knows*. How can he possibly know?

'How did I know?' He reads my mind. 'I have a camera in my house.' He holds his phone up. 'Linked to my phone. I knew you were in there as soon as I got to work, just had to wait for a chance to get away and catch you.'

He doesn't even seem bothered that I've been in his house. Why would he have a camera in his house? Apart from the TV there's only old, rickety furniture, nothing worth stealing.

'It's disguised as a hook in the hallway. Very clever getting your friend to push his way in when he did, otherwise I'd have caught you red-handed. I'd be interested to know how you got in.'

I look down at my hands and say nothing.

Thankfully, he sits back in his chair. 'I'm guessing

that you sneaked in when I was putting the bin out. I can't think of any other way you'd have got in.'

I take a deep breath, I mustn't let him distract me from what I have to say but before I can say anything he laughs.

'Okay, don't tell me. But I'll admit I'm surprised. I didn't think you had it in you.'

In spite of my anger I can feel my face growing hot, like a naughty school kid getting a telling off.

'Josie.' He leans forward again and looks at me with those eyes that I'd thought so kind and deep. 'I can't understand what you've done, or why. You know how I feel about you and what really puzzles me is, if you wanted to know something why didn't you just ask?'

This isn't how the conversation is supposed to be going; *he* should be justifying himself, not me.

'You stalked my mother.' I stare into his eyes. 'You pestered her with your phone calls and you made her life miserable.'

He does look shocked now.

'What are you talking about?' The colour has drained from his face and the smile has gone.

'I saw the birthday card you sent her. I recognised your writing. Don't bother denying it.'

He looks puzzled for a moment and then recovers himself.

'No, no, no.' He shakes his head. 'You've got this all wrong. I know you don't want to hear it but we were in love, she was going to leave him and come and live with me.'

'No, she wasn't!' I shout at him. 'It was all in your mind, you're sick. You need help.'

'What makes you think I was stalking her? Whatever gave you that idea? I know you don't want to think badly of your mother and you don't want to accept it but the fact is, we were in a relationship and if she hadn't died, she would be with me now.' He sits back and crosses his arms. 'I'm sorry, that's just the way it was and you need to accept that.'

'You've lied to me all this time. When I was talking about Mum you knew what you'd done. You made me talk about her even though I didn't want to. You encouraged me to think the worst of her and I'll never forgive myself for letting you.'

Adam shakes his head with a sad smile.

'Josie, I haven't lied and I think you know that. You're just trying to convince yourself.'

'No. You're a liar and I'm going to the police, I'm going to tell them what I found in your house.'

For the first time he looks afraid and I think; I *am* right and maybe this will work, maybe the police *will* believe me.

'I saw the scarf,' I say. 'I saw Mum's scarf hanging in your hallway. I know you took it.'

He looks down at the floor for a moment and I can see his mouth working as if he's trying to compose himself. He seems shaken and I wonder if he's going to confess everything but when he looks up at me he gives a croaky laugh and shakes his head as if to tell me how unbelievable I am.

'What does that prove Josie? It proves that your mother came to my house. Remember? You, yourself, thought she was having an affair, you were convinced of it.'

'Only until I found out the truth.'

'A very convenient truth wasn't it? You must realise that your father made up the stalking story to spare your feelings.'

I can see now that this is pointless; he's never going to admit anything. I'm so confused but I'm certain that mum would never cheat. Why did I ever, ever doubt her? I so hate myself for even *thinking* that she could do such a thing.

'Just tell me why, why did you pretend to have feelings for me?' I have to know but I hate the way it came out; I sound pathetic and needy.

He looks surprised at my question and for a moment he reminds me of the Adam that I thought I was falling in love with.

'I didn't pretend, Josie. I *do* have feelings for you. Everything I said to you was true. I would never lie to you.'

What did I think he'd say? Not that.

'We can forget all of this, nothing needs to change between us. We can sort this out. I forgive you for breaking into my house, I know you were just confused.' He looks at me and smiles.

'Forgive me?' I shout at him. 'I may have sneaked into your house but what you've done is far, far worse and I'll *never* forgive you.' But there's a part of me wants to believe him, part of me wishes I'd never remembered that card. Ignorance is bliss.

'And you should never have been my counsellor, you must have known who I was when you saw my name. Why? Why would you do that?'

'I know and I'm sorry, and that was wrong of me but I wanted to help. For Nessa's sake. And when I started to have feelings for you, I did try to stop the sessions, you know I did. Although I couldn't tell you the real reason.'

'Josie,' he reaches over and takes my hand in his but I snatch my hand away. 'Don't touch me! I'm going to the police!'

'Please don't.' Is that fear I can see in his eyes?

'BIRO!' I shout as loudly as I can. 'BIRO! COME OUT!'

Biro bursts out from his hiding place and Adam looks at him in shock.

'I've recorded everything.' Biro holds his phone up to Adam.

'Recorded what?' Adam laughs. 'That I was having an affair with Josie's mother?'

'That's bollocks and you know it and at the very least you'll be sacked for hitting on someone you're supposed to be counselling.' Biro walks over to us and looms over Adam. Adam jumps up from the chair and Biro is forced to step back. Adam glares at Biro; they're almost the same height. Biro jabs his finger towards Adam's face. 'You'd better start looking for a new job, mate, 'cos you're done here.'

Adam grabs Biro's hand and steps closer to him.

'Watch who you're pointing at, *mate*.'

They stare are each other menacingly and I hold my breath.

Adam suddenly lets go of Biro's hand and laughs then shrugs his shoulders and turns away from Biro and walks over to the door. As he opens the door he turns around and smiles sadly at me.

'Sorry it had to end like this, Josie, we could have had something special together.'

I watch as he walks out of the room and hear his footsteps fading away down the corridor.

Biro and I look at each other.

'What are we going to do now, Biro.' My voice sounds hollow.

'Mate.' Biro runs a hand through his hair. 'I haven't

got a fucking clue.'

Chapter 26

Josie

In the end we did the only thing that we could do; we told Dad.

I knew that if Biro and I went to the police we'd have a hard time convincing them that Adam was the stalker and we'd just sound like a couple of hysterical teenagers. And even if we'd gone to the police, I couldn't have kept that from Dad, anyway.

It was horrible telling Dad all about Adam and how I thought I was in love with him. Beyond embarrassing.

I'm still not sure about Adam; I can't help it, he was so convincing. I don't doubt for a minute that he was stalking Mum but what if he didn't *realise* he was stalking her? He must be ill, mustn't he? Because he sounded so believable that he must truly believe they were in a relationship. I keep telling myself that it was just a crush but it's hard to just turn off my feelings – one minute I hate him and the next I want to forgive him.

Dad didn't need any convincing about going to the police, he thinks Adam is dangerous and needs to be stopped. I don't know what the police will do – Adam has Mum's scarf but I can't see them arresting him.

Although, Dad says that they'll take us seriously because they'd reported it to them in the months before she died.

Dad is absolutely furious that I've been into Adam's house.

I didn't want to tell him that bit but there was really no way around it; how could I tell him about the scarf if I hadn't been in Adam's house? I thought about lying but then I thought there have been too many lies and things unsaid so I may as well just confess and get it over with.

And I couldn't think of a believable lie either; and it'll all come out anyway because we'll have to tell the police and I'm not looking forward to that.

As soon as we'd finished telling Dad, Biro played the recording. Dad wouldn't look at me when he was listening to it; he just looked at the floor but I could see his face was flushed and I thought he was going to cry.

I felt like a traitor; twice a week I was having cosy meetings with Mum's stalker and fancying myself in love with him and Dad had to listen to me admitting that I thought she'd had an affair. That was the worst part for me.

There was silence when the recording finished and I thought, *he hates me*. But Dad got up from the chair and came over and pulled me into his arms. He hugged me tight and said how sorry he was and I said *Dad, I'm the one who's sorry* and he said, *you have nothing to be sorry about, I should have been there for you.*

We stood there for quite a while and then Biro made a coughing sound and Dad let me go and I sat back down.

Dad went over and picked the phone up and rang the police. He was talking to them for ages and got put on hold for a long time and then finally got put through to the right person.

When he'd finished telling them they said they were coming to talk to us and I couldn't believe it when they're turned up about an hour later.

There were two of them, WPC Roper, I think, and a Detective Inspector Peters. They both seemed very nice, not disbelieving at all. The WPC wrote everything down in her notebook (she must have very small writing) while DI Peters asked the questions. He didn't say anything when I told him how I got into Adam's house, just raised an eyebrow.

We went through everything about a million times and Biro had to do something with the recording so they could have a copy of it. There was something about not being able to use it in court and I was shocked then, because I just thought they'd give Adam a telling off and make him promise not to do it again. When I said that to Biro after they'd gone he couldn't stop laughing, said something about what an innocent I was. I got really stroppy with him and said I'm not an innocent and he laughed even more.

I could hit him sometimes.

Anyway, the police left after about two hours and said that they'd keep us informed. Biro and I have to go into the station in the next week and give a formal statement and I can't say that I'm looking forward to that. I can't help thinking that we're wasting our time, when it comes down to it it's our word against his and they haven't got any actual *proof* of what he'd done. It's not like we even have the birthday card anymore.

'Well, we've done all we can, it's up to them now, it's in their hands.' Dad said as he closed the front door on them. 'That Peters bloke really reminds me of someone but I can't think who.'

'That's Louise's partner, you know, Louise who works with Uncle Ralph,' I said.

'Really?' He'll be the one that caught the Frogham Throttler.' He looks pleased. 'So they must be taking us seriously.'

'That's good isn't it?' I try to sound confident but I don't feel it.

'It certainly is. Right, that's enough of all that for one day.' He rubs his hands together. 'I don't know about you two but I'm starving. Shall we get a takeaway? Indian? Thai? Chinese?'

'Thai.' Biro and I say in unison.

'Thai it is,' says Dad as he roots through the magazine rack for the takeaway menu. He produces the dog-eared menu with a flourish.

'Tell me what you want and I'll ring it through.'

We give Dad our order and he gets on the phone to *Bang Thai Dee* and forgets what we've told him and just orders pretty much everything on the menu.

'Ten-past-nine, going to be up all night with indigestion,' Dad says, looking at his watch. He sounds cheerful and upbeat but I know it's for my benefit; I know when he's acting.

Dad goes out to the kitchen and Biro and I sit in silence listening to the sound of Dad rattling around, clattering plates, opening a drawer and knives and forks being pulled out.

'Wonder if they'll go straight to his house and search it?' I say.

'Hope so. Though they'll probably need a search warrant. They probably won't find anything because you searched it and never found anything and if he's got any sense he'll have got rid of the scarf by now.'

'Of course he will.' I feel suddenly depressed and dejected; do I want him to go to prison? I don't know what I want. 'He's going to get away with it, isn't he?'

'Maybe,' says Biro grimly. 'But at the very least he'll lose his job. Stop him grooming anyone else.'

'Don't say grooming, it sounds horrible.'

'That's what it is.'

'I know now it was just a stupid crush, how could I possibly think I knew someone after so little time with them? I'm an idiot.' I fight back tears.

'No, you're not.' Dad comes into the lounge and puts the plates and cutlery on the coffee table. 'You're human, like the rest of us, and *he* took advantage of that. You've nothing to blame yourself for at all.' He sits down on the sofa and puts his arm around me. I give him a shaky smile. 'The main thing is that he's been caught now and he'll have to pay the price for what he's done.'

'He will,' I say.

'Too right,' says Biro.

'Hopefully he'll get a prison sentence,' I say, not knowing if I mean it.

'Lose his job at the least,' says Biro.

The doorbell interrupts us and Dad jumps up and goes out to the hallway and reappears with two huge, brown carrier bags, a delicious smell drifting out of them. He brings the bags in and pulls out assorted foil containers and arranges them all on the coffee table. We prise the lids off and heap spoonfuls onto our plates.

I take a mouthful of chicken and it tastes like sawdust in my mouth. I was starving but now my hunger has vanished and I know I'm not going to be able to eat a thing. I push the food around a bit to disguise it and make it look like I'm eating something; I don't want to spoil Biro and Dad's meal.

Biro catches my eye. 'Not hungry?'

'Thought I was, but, you know...' I trail off.

'I can't eat it either.' Dad puts his knife and fork across his full plate. 'Can't get it down.'

'Nor me.' Biro puts his plate on the table, he hasn't eaten anything either.

Skipper is sitting to attention with his eyes fixed on our plates but I don't think he'll be getting any; he was sick all over the carpet last time.

'Okay.' Dad gets up from the sofa. 'I'll go and get the clingfilm.'

Chapter 27

Josie

The weekend crawled by in centimetres. I think the three of us were expecting something to happen; for Adam to be arrested, or at least arrested and released. Biro texted me every five minutes asking if there was any news. We were waiting for *something*.

Instead we got nothing. We heard nothing at all from the police and by Sunday night Dad was itching to ring them and find out if anything had happened. I think because they came out so quickly, we expected them to have it all wrapped up in a day. I managed to persuade him not to ring them; said that they'd promised they'd keep us informed and that if there was anything to tell us they'd let us know and we didn't want to look like pests.

But the real reason I didn't want him to ring them is that I'm sure it's going to be bad news. Adam will talk his way out of it and there's no proof of anything so he'll just get away with it. He might not even lose his job – although there is the recording so maybe he will because of his relationship with me. Grooming, as Biro keeps telling me.

We pottered around the house pretending we

weren't waiting for news and on Sunday morning I heard Dad on the phone in his bedroom. I'm sure he was telling Uncle Ralph everything; they're pretty close even though they deny it and he'd be the first person he'd confide in. He kept his voice low and the door was closed so I couldn't really make out what he was saying, even though I was listening outside, but I'm pretty sure he was crying. I probably shouldn't have done that – listened outside – but I was worried about him.

When he came out I asked him if he was okay and he said of course he was. I grabbed his arm and stopped him from disappearing downstairs and told him that he wasn't fooling me and that if we're going to start living our lives properly, we need to be honest with each other and to stop pretending everything's alright when it's not. He tried to do the *everything's alright* thing but could see I wasn't having any of it so eventually admitted that since it all came out on Friday he's been struggling. He's been trying to hold it together for me but it's bought everything back. He says he blames himself for not being able to stop the stalking when Mum was alive.

We went downstairs and had a good long talk about it and I said there's only one person to blame and that's Adam. And as I said it, I realised it was true. We need to stop thinking that we're somehow to blame. I think we both felt better for talking things through and we've both agreed – no more secrets.

Dad said I should stay off college for a few days but I disagreed; I want to get back to normal, whatever that is. Only me and Biro know about it so it's not as if I'll have to talk about it or explain myself to anyone else.

I do feel so sad, sad for Mum, for Dad, and myself. But we have to remember – and I said this to Dad –

that the stalking part was only a small amount of time in our lives and we mustn't let it spoil all of the happy years that we had. Dad laughed and said I had *an old head on young shoulders,* whatever that means.

Also, a part of me is sad about Adam. Why does it have to be that the first time I actually feel as if I'm falling in love it has to be with a stalker? But I'll get over it; if nothing else I'm in a much better place than I was a year ago.

I've deleted Adam's phone number and all of his texts; although they were all very business-like. I can see now that he was very careful not to incriminate himself. I don't think he would text me but I want to make sure *I* don't text *him.*

I'm not intending to, but now I *can't.*

So. On Monday morning I went to college and went to all of my classes and everything was as it's always been and I felt surprising okay. In a way it almost seems as if the events of the last few days never happened because everything feels so unreal. I can't believe that I had the guts to sneak into Adam's house. Maybe that's another side of me; the one that's on YouTube singing Wonderwall.

Ellie, Biro and I were sitting at our usual table at lunchtime, eating and chatting, about nothing really, just a normal day. I watched Biro wolfing down a Panini and I suddenly thought; I have a good life. I have family and friends and I am going to pass my exams and no matter what, Dad and I *will* be okay.

And then a split second after I thought that, I saw them; the police.

Biro saw them first. Ellie started talking about some hench guy who's in her social studies class; I think she's trying to make Biro jealous but it's lost on him.

Anyway, Biro gave me a look across the table which Ellie never noticed but I saw Biro's eyes flick to the windows behind me. My heart started pounding then because I thought for a moment that he meant Adam was outside.

When I came in to the cafeteria, I'd scanned the room, afraid that Adam was in there and I didn't know what I was going to do if I saw him. Surely, he wouldn't be at work if they'd arrested him?

I turned around, trying to look casual and saw there was a police car parked up in front of the entrance and the figures of WPC Roper and DI Peters were walking into Reception.

'You alright, Josie?' Ellie looked at me with concern. 'You look very pale.'

'Yeah, I'm fine.' I pasted a big, fake smile on my face. 'Stayed up too late watching telly is all.'

'Tell me about it,' she says. 'Think I need to get my telly moved out of my room if I want to pass any exams.'

She laughs and I join in but inside I'm thinking; if the police are here maybe he's been arrested, maybe we'll hear something soon.

We finished lunch and left the cafeteria for our next class and the police car was still there and I couldn't stop thinking about it for the next two hours, imagining what was happening. The time ticked by so slowly I thought I'd go mental.

After what seemed like forever it was finally time to go home and I met Biro in front of the admin office where we usually meet. We walked straight around to Reception to see if the police car was still there but of course it was gone.

I didn't know whether to be relieved or disappointed

and nor did Biro. He waved me off as I got onto the bus and I know he feels the same as me: in limbo. What if they never arrest or charge him? Biro said that he'd seen the police outside Adam's parent's house at the weekend and I wondered why they were there because he doesn't even live with them anymore.

I was in such a daze that I nearly missed my stop and just about managed to ring the bell in time. It was chucking it down with rain and I pulled the hood of my Parka up and sprinted the short distance from the bus stop to home. I turned the corner into my street and the first thing I saw was the police car parked outside our house.

Here we go: news at last.

Chapter 28

Josie

I put my key in the lock but before I can turn it the front door is yanked opened by Dad.

'Josie, sweetheart, the police are here.'

He seems keyed up and out of breath. I study his face; he looks tired. And worried.

I take my Parka off and take it out into the kitchen and drape it over the chair to dry. Even while I'm doing it, I know that I'm putting it off; hearing what the police are going to say. What is it I don't want to hear? That they've caught him or not caught him?

I have no idea.

I take my boots off and place them on the mat by the back door and then follow Dad into the lounge. DI Peters is standing by the window and WPC Roper is sitting in one of the armchairs balancing a teacup on her knee. The teacup looks toy-like against the size of her legs and I realise how big she is. Not fat, just large, super-sized, like a giant. She doesn't look comfortable at all.

They both greet me with wary smiles and I sit down on the sofa and Dad sits next to me.

'We've just been bringing your dad up to date about

the developments.' DI Peters sits down in the seat opposite us and leans forward with his arms resting on his knees.

There's an uncomfortable silence and I guess what he's going to say next: there's no evidence and Adam's talked his way out of it.

'Mr Borden has not been to the college or returned to his house since Friday and as yet we've been unable to locate him.'

DI Peters looks at Dad then looks at me.

'But we have, erm, discovered certain facts about him.'

'What sort of facts?' I have to say it twice because the first time it comes out in a whisper.

'The fact is, Adam Borden is not a counsellor and never has been. From our enquiries it appears that he worked for a few months at the college as an office temp before he was sacked two weeks ago. From his time working there he had access to student files and was involved in making appointments for the counselling staff.'

I look at DI Peters dumbly and he continues.

'It seems reasonable to assume that he saw your name had been put forward for counselling and removed it from the list so an appointment wasn't made in the normal way. He then passed himself off as your counsellor.'

I'm stunned. *Everything* about Adam was a lie. 'But how could he? Why? I don't understand.'

'The room where you had your counselling sessions was an unused office which was due for refurbishment. He simply took the key and we assume he had another one cut so that he could come and go at will. Whilst he was still employed by the college, he would slip away from the office for half-an-hour and meet you in the disused office. Once he'd been dismissed, he never returned his security pass and simply used it to enter the college whenever he liked. As to why he did it we can only speculate.'

I'm having trouble thinking straight. The room, the old calendar, the dusty boxes, it all makes a kind of sense. Why didn't I suspect? It all seems so obvious now. I remember Adam often arrived out of breath as if he'd been running. He must have made excuses to slip out of the office to see me; that's why he could never stay late. And the excuses of urgent meetings with other clients – all lies that he told so easily, and lies that I believed so easily. But why would I doubt him?

'The college will, of course, be reviewing their security arrangements in light of what's happened.'

'Why was he sacked?' I interrupt. 'What did he do?'

DI Peters clears his throat.

'A female tutor reported him for inappropriate behaviour. Apparently, they went out on a date but when she refused to see him again he wouldn't leave her alone. She started to receive telephone calls from him, he sent flowers to her home and insisted that they were in a relationship. She also suspected he was following her but she couldn't be sure. Classic stalking behaviour. Eventually the temping agency were informed and his contract was terminated. Although by then the stalking had stopped.'

DI Peters doesn't say it but he doesn't have to. It stopped because he was counselling me and I was going to take her place. The argument in the cafeteria, he told me she was hassling *him*, wouldn't take no for an answer. More lies.

'Did he temp at Straitleys?' demands Dad. 'Is that

where he...' his voice trails off but I know what he was going to say; is that where he targeted Mum? Did he see her at work and decide she was going to be next? Did Mum *know* him? Had she worked with him?

'Yes, he did, Mr Sparkes. He worked there briefly in Reception for several weeks as holiday cover. As you know Straitleys is a huge building and we think that he probably saw your late wife as she passed through Reception. There is no indication that he had any contact with her or with the office where she worked.'

So they've checked. I don't know why it matters but I'm glad that Mum never knew him.

'What happens now?' Dad asks.

'We've applied for a warrant to search his house and we should have it by tomorrow lunchtime.'

'Maybe he's hiding in his house,' I say. 'He could be, if you haven't been able to search it and you can't find him.'

DI Peters shakes his head. 'No. He's not there, the landlord has a key and one of our officers accompanied him into the house. All of the signs were that Adam Borden had left in a hurry.'

'His father and stepmother live in the next street,' I say. 'Don't they know where he is?' I know they've been there because Biro saw them.

'We have spoken to them and they've had no contact with him recently. They've been estranged from Adam Borden for quite some time and very rarely see him even though he lives near to them.'

'I know they stopped speaking when his father remarried.' Why do I even care?

DI Peters looks confused. 'No, his father hasn't remarried, his parents are still together. Whatever gave you the idea he'd remarried?'

So that was a lie too.

'Adam told me his mother died when he was seventeen,' I say flatly.

'Ah. I see.' DI Peters nods thoughtfully.

'Bastard.' Dad mutters under his breath.

'As soon as the search has been done, we'll inform you of any developments but until then I would ask that if he makes any contact at all that you inform us immediately.'

'Do you think he will? Is he dangerous? Because if he is, I want police protection for Josie,' Dad demands.

'Please, Mr Sparkes,' soothes DI Peters. 'There are no indications at all that he's dangerous but we would advise against speaking or having any contact with him. No matter how persuasive or genuine he may appear.'

That's directed at me; he thinks I'm a stupid, infatuated little girl who still might be sweet talked by him. What a complete idiot I must look.

DI Peters stands up and WPC Roper attempts to pull herself out of the chair that she's wedged in. We all look away in embarrassment while she huffs and puffs. Skipper watches and backs into the corner. I think he's afraid she's going to fall on him.

'We'll be in touch.' DI Peters nods at Dad and I and goes out into the hallway. WPC Roper has managed to get to her feet and squeezes past the coffee table and follows DI Peters. Dad and I jump up and watch from the front door as they climb into the police car and drive off.

'Well,' says Dad as he closed the door, 'Let's hope by this time tomorrow they can find some evidence and track him down and arrest him.'

Fingers crossed.

Chapter 29

Josie

The police didn't come back the next day, but they did phone Dad to say that they would be visiting us on Wednesday. Dad went into super protective mode and insisted on driving me to college and picking me up afterwards. He's insistent that until Adam is found he doesn't want to take any chances and he doesn't want me going anywhere on my own.

I've told him that he's being ridiculous but he won't listen. I think Adam needs help and what he's done is wrong, obviously, but I'm sure he wouldn't hurt me or anyone else. I think he's mentally ill. Dad says it's better to be safe than sorry and because he's had enough to worry about, I've given in and gone along with it. It makes a change from waiting for the bus, I suppose.

Dad picks me up and we've just got home and taken our coats off when the doorbell rings and through the opaque window I can see the outlines of DI Peters and WPC Roper. I open the door and as they come in, I'm pretty sure that every curtain in the street is twitching at the sight of a police car parked outside our house, again.

We all troop into the lounge and sit down and Dad

and I look at DI Peters expectantly. They must have made some progress otherwise they wouldn't be here. WPC Roper hands DI Peters a cardboard file and he opens it, studies the contents for a few minutes and then takes out several sheets of paper.

'We obtained a search warrant and a thorough search of Adam Borden's house was conducted yesterday and certain items were found and removed as evidence.'

'What did they find?' Dad's voice is hoarse.

I want to know. I don't want to know.

DI Peters looks down at the sheet of paper in his hand. 'A woman's scarf,' he reads, 'A large quantity of photographs and two items of women's jewellery.'

'Where did you find all this? Was it hidden?' I suddenly need to know. I searched that house and found nothing.

'The scarf was hanging on a peg in the hallway and the other items were found in the loft. The loft walls had been used as a sort of makeshift gallery and the photographs were pasted onto the plasterboard cladding. No attempt had been made to hide the photographs or the jewellery.'

Dad and I look at each other in shock.

'The photographs,' DI Peters continues, 'Were mostly of the late Mrs Sparkes and one other as yet, unidentified woman although there were several of you, Josie. The photographs all appeared to have been taken using a mobile phone and without the subject's knowledge, probably when there were going about their normal, daily business.'

I feel sick. I steel a look at Dad and he looks ashen. We knew he was the stalker, but photographs?

DI Peter's hands over two plastic evidence bags, 'Do

you recognise either of these items?'

Dad takes the bags and we stare at them much longer than necessary. There's a silver coloured charm type bracelet and a small oval locket with a broken chain. Neither of them is Mum's. Where did Adam get them from? *Who* did he get them from?

'No.' Dad says with relief, handing the bags back. 'I don't recognise them.'

'Josie?' asked DI Peters.

'No. I don't recognise them either. They're not mine or Mum's.'

'Thank you,' DI Peters tucks them back inside the cardboard folder. 'We've put out an alert to ascertain the whereabouts of Adam Borden and this has been extended to other forces throughout the country. He doesn't have his passport with him so we're confident that we'll have him in custody before very long.'

'I hope so,' says Dad. 'Because you haven't caught him yet, have you? Even if you do, he'll probably get off with a slap on the wrist and a fine,' Dad says gloomily.

DI Peters clears his throat.

'I'm afraid that's not all that we've discovered about Adam Borden.'

Dad and I look at DI Peters in alarm.

'What? What have you discovered?'

'In view of recent developments, we decided to review the CCTV footage taken at the tube station on the day of your wife's death.'

An unfathomable look passes between DI Peters and WPC Roper and I suddenly don't want to hear what he has to say; what I know he's going to say. I want to clap my hands over my ears and pretend none of this is happening.

'Amongst the people on the platform – and there were a great many people waiting that day, we've clearly identified that Adam Borden was present at the time of your wife's death. Now, please don't jump to conclusions because this doesn't mean that he was involved in your wife's death. We have to investigate all avenues and we wouldn't be doing our jobs properly if we didn't consider the fact that Adam Borden was there.'

'He could have pushed her,' Dad's in shock and his voice comes out in a whisper. 'Why else would he be there?'

'Please, Mr Sparkes, don't jump to conclusions. He was stalking your wife but we've no reason to suspect that he's violent. He followed her and watched her and it may well be that's all he was doing but we need to investigate further to be sure.'

Dad shakes his head.

'No. I know. That bastard killed her. He pushed her.'

Chapter 30

Josie

We're going on holiday.

Dad and I are going to Spain to stay with Nanny and Grandad. It's the first time we'll have been to visit them since Mum died although they've asked us loads of times. We couldn't face going without Mum but we have to move on now, lay the ghosts I think they call it.

We're going next week which means I'll be taking some time off from college but to be honest it's not like it'll affect my exams; it's not as if I need to swot up or anything. I'm not going to panic and go blank this time either because I feel quite chilled about it. With everything else that's happened since I last took them, I can't understand why I got in such a state last time.

Dad has booked the flights but he's only booked them one way. He says we might fancy staying a bit longer than a couple of weeks and he's got lots of holidays to use up so why not? *See how we feel* is what he said.

He's not fooling me though, I know the real reason he wants to go; he won't be happy until Adam is tracked down and locked up so he can't get anywhere near me. He's got it into his head that Adam murdered

Mum even though the police haven't any evidence that he did, although they're still looking into it. So far, they're saying that it wasn't anything but a tragic accident but Dad doesn't agree and says it could be the perfect murder. Dad says it would be impossible to prove unless he was caught on camera, which he wasn't, and someone would have seen him if he pushed her.

Me and Dad have had such long talks about it all; at least he's not bottling things up now and nor am I. Dad says stalking is a classic cycle – first there's attraction which if not returned soon turns to obsession and then the last stage is destruction. Or murder. It doesn't always end like that though does it? Not every stalker is a murderer. I've done a bit of Googling too and it's very rare for a stalker to turn into a murderer. Adam stalked the tutor at college and he didn't murder her, did he? I think Dad's just getting a bit carried away.

He wants someone to blame for Mum's death.

I don't think for one minute that Adam had anything to do with Mum's death. It doesn't make sense for him to have killed her – he was obsessed with her but he loved her in his own twisted way. I know he stalked her and that was so wrong but I'm sure he didn't have anything to do with her death and I can't bring myself to be afraid of him. But I will be glad when he's caught because he needs help.

Dad can never forgive him for what he put Mum and us through but once I'd recovered from the shock, I felt surprisingly alright. I've amazed myself. I've gone over those counselling sessions a million times in my head, analysing them to see if I should have guessed, if I was a gullible fool.

Maybe if I hadn't had a massive crush on him, I would have been suspicious – or would I? I had no reason to doubt him, I thought he was a counsellor and never having seen a counsellor before I had nothing to compare him with. And anyway, you can't go through life suspecting everyone and everything.

Well you can, but I don't intend to.

So, I'm going along with the holiday thing because I want Dad to stop fretting. I want to see the frown marks between his eyebrows disappear and I want my old, jolly Dad back, the one who always looks on the bright side and does mental things like wear swimming goggles to chop onions. I also want to see Nanny and Grandad again because it's ages since we've seen them and I've missed them. And they're so excited that we're going because they've missed us too. I know it's going to be hard for all of us without Mum there but we'll get through it. We have to.

We haven't told them about the Adam business; no point in them worrying and being upset as well. They're still coming to terms with Mum's death and I can't bear to put them through any more pain, and what would it gain by telling them? Absolutely nothing. Once we're on that flight the agreement is that we don't mention *him* or any of it, we'll be like, it never happened.

I'll miss Biro and Ellie but they'll still going to be here when I get back. We're friends and they're not going to stop being my friends just because I've been on holiday for a while, are they? Biro is looking after Skipper while we're away; apparently his Mum really wants a dog but his dad Charlie says it's not practical. Biro says she thinks having Skipper for a while will get his dad used to the idea and he'll give in and they'll get one.

I have a feeling that Ellie and Biro might be more than friends by the time I come back, although they both try to make out they don't know what I'm talking about whenever I mention it.

We'll see.

So. Mum. If you're looking down from wherever you are; don't worry.

We miss you like mad and we always will.

But we're going to be okay.

Chapter 31

Adam

Stalker.

That was what hurt the most; when Josie called me a stalker. I knew then that there was no going back. I've seen that look before and it never ends well. My parents gave me that look many times; they dressed it up with *we only want to help* or *we're trying to understand you* but they couldn't hide it; the disgust.

And when that lanky idiot friend of hers jumped out from behind the cupboard and started on about the police and recording me and all that bollocks, well I knew then that it really was all over.

So here I am; can't go home because my slimy landlord is showing the police around my house – the house I pay over the top rent for because I couldn't get a reference and apparently, I can't do a thing about it. It was sheer luck that I was out when they arrived although I wish I'd been prepared. I wish I had more than the clothes I'm standing up in. And they'll find my keepsakes and my photographs and make it dirty and criminal and I can never go back there now.

Didn't I help Josie? Yes, I did. She was in a right mess when I found her and now she's a different person, all fixed.

Because of me.

I might not be a counsellor but I helped her so what's the difference? My intentions were good; when I saw her name, I wanted to help her, for Nessa's sake. Although when I first met Josie it was a bit of a shock – I never considered how much she would look like Nessa.

But it's all ruined now; Josie and I had something *real* and we could have been happy together but she had to go and ruin it and now she looks at me the way everyone else does and it's too *late*.

I'm a good-looking guy and I never have any trouble getting a date but other people just see it all *wrong*, they don't understand.

Nessa was *the one*. The first time I saw her she took my breath away.

So beautiful.

And that smile. She looked over at me and smiled and said *goodnight* and that was it; love at first sight. We both felt it, I could see it in her eyes. I'd hated temping at Straitleys but meeting Nessa changed that. I even used to get into work early to make sure I was there when she arrived. I begged to stay when the woman I was covering for came back from maternity leave, but there wasn't a vacancy and so I had to leave. I so missed seeing Nessa every day.

If it hadn't been for *him* things would have been so different; she felt sorry for him because he was old and past it and Nessa was so sweet and loyal. She should have been more selfish.

It was only a matter of time before we would have been together properly and then we wouldn't have to use our secret signals to tell each other our deepest feelings. I can only imagine how happy she felt when she opened my birthday card; I was there that day, watching from across the road behind a parked van. I saw them all leave the house and go out celebrate her birthday and I knew that she was only pretending to enjoy it for their sakes.

I should have been taking her out; *I* should have been the one giving her presents. We were biding our time; waiting for the right moment for Nessa to leave him.

Nessa would still be here now if it wasn't for *him*.

When Nessa and I were properly together I would've looked after her and she'd have been *safe*. She wouldn't have needed to work and see other people, we'd have each other and that would be enough. More than enough.

If she'd been with me, she'd still be here and I can't forgive *him* for that; it's his fault Nessa's gone.

I would have kept Josie safe, too.

But not now.

It's too late now.

So here I am; standing on Frogly-by-Sea's run-down pier in the driving rain and I can never go home because the police will never understand.

The sky is dark grey and I'm soaking wet and as I gaze out at the grey swirling sea, I remember the look on Nessa's face the last time I saw her.

And I wish I could forget.

I'd followed her to the station that morning, as I usually did, because I was looking after her. But that day I'd decided; enough was enough and she had to leave *him* and start her new life with me and start putting *us* first.

I was standing a few feet behind her, rehearsing the

speech in my head that was going to make her see sense. Nessa was at the front, near the platform, doing her usual thing of pretending that she didn't know I was there. We had this telepathic thing you know; she *knew* I was there even though she hadn't seen me and she started looking around her like she always did because she couldn't stop herself from trying to find me.

And then the person in front of me moved slightly and she saw me and our eyes locked; her eyes widened and her mouth opened in an *oh* expression. And I couldn't help myself; I smiled at her, our special secret smile. She looked away then as if she hadn't seen me; playing our game of pretending we were strangers. She took her scarf off for some reason, I don't know why and then she turned back and looked at me again but she wasn't smiling. Something had frightened her; I could see it in her eyes. She turned away and the next thing I knew she stumbled and fell forward.

I can't think about it.

I can't bear to.

Blue and pink swirls. Robins.

I didn't even realise that I had it until I returned home. I have no memory of picking up her scarf or of leaving the station; no recollection of how I got home. I was in such a state of shock that I lay curled up on the floor of the lounge all day and through the night; stricken with grief and unable to move.

How did I carry on?

I have no idea; life was unbearable without Nessa but somehow, I got through the days. Meeting Josie was fate, it was meant to be.

But now she hates me, just like everyone else.

My hands are wet and cold and the wind is whipping freezing rain into my face and I can hear someone shouting.

'Hey! Are you okay?'

I turn my head and six feet behind me there's a woman huddled in a quilted coat clutching the lead of a bedraggled Yorkshire terrier.

I stare at her for a moment and wonder what she wants.

'Are you okay?' she shouts, 'Can I help? You're very close to the edge.'

I look down at my feet and see that I'm on the outside of the pier railings; the tips of my shoes are suspended over the swirling waves and my hands are clutching the railing behind me.

'Climb back over the railing. Nothing's that bad, we can talk about it, maybe I can help.'

I look at her and smile and she stares at me in surprise. If only she knew how many times I've heard those same words.

And I realise that there is a way to be with Nessa again; it's so blindingly simple I can't believe I didn't think of it before.

I close my eyes and jump.

Epilogue

'Who found him?'

'Dog walker. He's waiting in the cafe.' PC Harris looked up at the bright blue painted window frames of the *Seadog Cafe*. Sitting in front of the car park on the promenade he wondered why they even bothered opening on a day like today. The ice cream shop next door was shuttered for the winter and he couldn't imagine they did much trade.

They were just shutting up shop for the day but the finding of a body made for good business. They'd served a handful of people all day but now every table was full.

The on-call police doctor squatted down on his haunches and studied the body. He pulled his coat around him as a light rain began to fall and the wind picked up speed. Seagulls wheeled and squawked as the sky darkened.

'How long do you think he's been in the sea?' Harris asked, frowning; the sooner they could get the body moved, the better. A small crowd of people had gathered on the promenade and he could see some of them holding mobile phones aloft.

'Hard to say until I've examined him but I'm

guessing not long. The fishes haven't started eating him and the clothes are in fairly good condition so I'd say a couple of days at the most. Any mispers match his description?'

'Not checked yet, the description's too broad. Be helpful if he had ID on him.' PC Harris could have looked before the doctor got here but there was no way he was touching a dead body. He shivered at the thought.

Dr Robertson tugged the zipper down on the leather jacket; the zipper jerked and snagged but once the jacket was open, he reached inside. Feeling around the lining of the jacket he felt for an inside pocket and finding it, pulled out a brown, water-bloated wallet. He stood up and handed it to Harris who took it and held it between his fingers and carefully peeled it open. He pulled out a card and squinted as he read it.

'Driving licence says Adam Borden, lived in Frogham.'

'Frogham? That's what, thirty miles away?'

'Yeah, about that.' Harris pulled an evidence bag from his pocket and dropped the wallet and card into it and sealed it. 'Which is a good thing, we can leave it to the local plod to tell the family. Can't stand those death visits.'

Dr Robertson directed his level gaze at the constable. 'Every cloud, eh?' he said sarcastically.

Harris looked puzzled, not sure if he was being got at.

'Do you want to see if the screens have arrived, constable? Or do you want me to conduct an examination with an audience watching?' Dr Robertson indicated the gathering crowd.

'Yes, sir, of course. I'll see to it.' Harris turned and

tramped off across the beach cursing his misfortune. Why did the dog walker have to catch him just as he was about to go off shift? He pulled his hat down over his eyes, but it offered little protection against the rain which was getting heavier by the minute.

'Move along please,' he shouted as he neared the crowd. 'Nothing to see here.'

THE END